# COL
# CHRISTMAS
## (Second Edition)

BY

AWARD-WINNING AND NATIONAL BESTSELLING AUTHOR

# Pat Simmons

ISBN-13:978-1537377216
ISBN-10:1537377213

# Dedication

*Couple by Christmas* is dedicated to my sisters-in-Christ of Victorious Ladies Reading Book Club. Thank you so much for your patience, love, and understanding.

# WHAT READERS ARE SAYING

5 Stars

"Heartwarming. A wonderful Christian novel about true love. I love the way the author intertwined scriptures into the story."—Angela on *A Baby for Christmas*

5 Stars

"Pat Simmons did it again! This book is full of love, life lessons and most importantly Christ." —Joyce N. on *A Noelle for Nathan*

5 Stars

"Simmons developed the characters so that I was drawn into their stories. I could feel every emotion." —Donnica Copeland, APOOO BookClub, Sista Talk Book Club, *Not Guilty of Love*

5 Stars

"This book is for *everyone* who feels there are no second chances in life. I always want to be a better person after reading her books—a better Christian, a better everything. This is truly a must-read book." —Theresa Cartwright Lands on *Crowning Glory*

# CHAPTER ONE

Derek Washington would be the first to admit he had been a jerk, but his ex-wife, Robyn, beat him to it. It didn't help that his own mother agreed with her.

Maybe it was the holidays or their son's upcoming sixth birthday on Christmas Day that had him re-evaluating his life. Lately, the what-ifs plagued him every time.

His divorce from Robyn had been ugly, mean-spirited, and anything but Christ-like. Their antics in the courtroom had caused the judge to decree they communicate through TalkingParents.com—a service designed to document their conversations—in case they returned to court for more litigation.

According to the parenting plan, the judge thought it best that they exchanged custody of Tyler at either of his grandparents' homes. Most of the time, Robyn's mother's house was the drop off and pick-up spot.

*"It's not your child that needs adult supervision, but the adults who are his parents," Judge Wilson had reprimanded them.*

Sitting behind his desk, Derek couldn't keep his

mind from drifting to that fateful day when he kissed his marriage goodbye. As a quality improvement manager for a Fortune 500 company in West St. Louis County, he had plenty of projects to keep him busy, but he lacked concentration.

At one time, he and Robyn had everything going for them; they were the epitome of a Christian couple at their church, Holy Ghost Temple. People complimented them as an attractive couple. They had the support of their respective in-laws who welcomed them as one of their own, which explained why his mother, Lane, and her mother, Sara, sat unified on the front row in court, giving both of them a disapproving glare once their marriage was dissolved.

It had been two years and he still had past regrets. Did Robyn?

"Stubborn people are fools," his mother stated on more than one occasion when he would drop by with Tyler. Of course, she made sure her grandson was distracted before she lit into Derek. "I know you still love Robyn or you would have moved on by now. Talk to her before *she* moves on. Don't repeat the same mistakes your foolish daddy did. Now, he's miserable with that other woman. *Hmphed*," she scolded him as if he were eleven years old instead of thirty—almost thirty-one.

Somehow, he made it through the day, operating on autopilot. Hours later, he hurried home to change before picking up Tyler for his weekend visit. He was almost out the door when he received an email alert from TalkingParents.com: I got Tyler from kindergarten instead of Mom. You can pick him up from my house.

Her house—formerly their house. Derek grunted. It had been months since they crossed paths. Their greetings were nothing more than cordial. Would time eventually heal the wounds between them so they could hold a civil conversation and not play the blame game?

After parking in front of the two-story, three-bedroom suburban house, he sat staring at the starter home they had purchased. Neighboring houses were lit from the porches to the trees. Not Robyn's. Besides the massive holiday wreath on the red door, the only other decorations were battery-operated candles that were displayed in all six front windows. Living in an apartment, his decorations were scarce too. *Be nice,* he prepped himself as he stepped out of his car, then strolled up the pathway and knocked.

"Daddy's here!" he heard Tyler scream from inside.

He grinned. At least someone was glad to see him.

"Get your hat and coat," Robyn said as she opened the door.

Rocking on his heels, Derek stayed rooted in place. The few times they had to alter the arrangements for pickups, she never invited him inside, so he never crossed the threshold—rain, shine, or blizzard.

She didn't make eye contact with him, but that didn't stop Derek from noticing everything about her. She was one pretty lady, which was what attracted him to her in the first place. Robyn still maintained her beauty. Her goldish-brown hair shone under the hallway light, and her skin glowed.

There was something else he noticed while she multi-tasked, bundling up their son and slipping her arm in the sleeve of her coat. She was fast, but not without him catching a glimpse of a Red Lobster uniform. Robyn was an executive assistant, so what was going on?

"You're working a second job? Why? I don't mind adjusting my child support amount," he offered with a frown. Money had been the source of many arguments. His wife loved to shop. He liked to save. But he wasn't going to be accusatory, not this time, not ever again. He had no say in her financial affairs unless it affected their child. What else was going on that he didn't know about?

"You're more than generous with your child support." She dismissed him when she knelt and opened her arms to receive a kiss and hug from their son. She stood again. "You can drop him off at my mother's." She guided Tyler outside.

"Bye, Mommy." He waved before latching on to Derek's hand. As they spun around to take the steps, he glanced over his shoulder. Robyn slowly closed the door without looking his way. He would give anything to earn her smile, a sparkle in her eyes, or her alluring tone when she used to tease him. Instead, he got nothing—no emotion.

Taking a deep breath, he continued to his car. He wanted to cross the line and break the "don't use the child as a pawn" rule to find out what Robyn was up to. He didn't.

As promised, Derek took his son to the park for ice skating. While going around the rink, he kept a grip on Tyler's hand while his mind stayed on Robyn. She had a liberal arts degree and could adapt to any working environment, but a waitress? No doubt, she had to be the prettiest one on staff. She could flirt without knowing it, and her shape...he groaned at the same time he almost fell, trying to steady Tyler.

Once they regained their rhythm, he thought about Robyn again. She was curvy and her pants did nothing to camouflage her God-given assets.

Forty-five minutes later, he hoped his son had worked up an appetite. "Hungry?" When Tyler bobbed his head, Derek grinned. He had a plan. "How about we go see Mommy at work?"

"Yeah." His eyes widened in excitement. "Are we going to see Granny Gibson too? Mommy takes me there when she has to work."

Hmm. That narrowed down the locations. "Not today. After we eat, you're going back home with me."

It was two weeks before Christmas, and he had planned to take his son to pick out his birthday present. That would have to wait until the next day. "Have you thought about what you want for your birthday?" Last year, Derek bought him a LEGO starter kit.

Since Robyn had Tyler last Christmas, he had to wait until the following weekend to play with him. That had to be the saddest Christmas of his life, and he wouldn't wish that same loneliness on anyone, but this year, Robyn would experience it.

"I want you to come live with us," Tyler stated matter-of-factly as he glanced out the window.

It was a good thing Tyler was strapped in because Derek jammed on his brakes at the same time the streetlight turned red. He eased his foot off and exhaled.

"Son, what's your second choice?" It would take a Christmas miracle for him and Robyn to reconcile for that to even be a possibility.

Robyn Washington couldn't be concerned about the stunned expression on her ex-husband's handsome face when he learned she had taken a second job—waitressing, at that. Under the hood of her long, thick lashes, she had a glimpse of what he was wearing. Black turtlenecks on Derek Washington should be outlawed. She chided herself for noticing.

It wasn't his business to know that her long-time position could be in jeopardy. The handwriting was on the wall about possible layoffs. When no one received Christmas bonuses, Robyn refused to cut back on her son's Christmas and birthday gifts. The job was seasonal and she planned to quit the day after Christmas, so she could celebrate a delayed birthday and Christmas with her son.

Until then, she would endure the constant walking and juggling of dishes. So far, the tips had been worth it.

Plus, shopping was her favorite pastime. Once she married, Robyn sometimes felt guilty about splurging. Then when Tyler was born, she and Derek practiced the Christian celebration of Christmas, which was to focus more on Christ than on spending on toys and other presents. That spiritual commitment was short lived, because they began to drift apart.

When her marriage ended, Robyn's faith faded. She went through the routine of being a Christian, but she felt like a failure. Only being a mother kept her going and distracted her from pity parties.

Her ex, Derek Tyler Washington, did make an exceptional father and was a good provider, never missing a child support payment or house note. Then last year, without warning, he started sending monthly maintenance checks for her—a perk that wasn't part of the divorce decree. She didn't call or text him, but logged on the message board and asked him why.

Because you're the mother of my
son.

After graciously thanking him, she had cried
that day—the first time in a long time. Robyn told
her best friend, she didn't know what to make of the
gesture.

"Maybe it's his way of saying he's sorry," Erica
Williams had suggested.

"Please. 'Sorry' is not in that man's vocabulary.
Maybe it's guilt from being a terrible husband."

"Well, count your blessings."

*Right.* She didn't trust her ex's motives. When
those blessings arrived like clockwork, she put them
in a savings account for Tyler. Her mistake was to
mention the money to her mother. Sara Gibson had
sung his praises. "I think you two got married too
soon and divorced even sooner."

It was an argument she would never win with
her mother, who was the die-hard captain of her ex-
husband's fan club. She was just as vocal about
Robyn's absences from church. "Why punish God
for your mistakes? Jesus is our best friend. Proverbs
21:24 says, 'He'll stick closer than any brother.'"

She once prided herself on her relationship with
God and had sought Him for wisdom in choosing a

mate. Robyn thought she heard His stamp of approval, so it took a while for her not to be angry with the Lord for her decision. Finally, she admitted marrying Derek had been a mistake. They weren't compatible.

Despite the disappointment, she was willing to give love a second chance in the future. There had to be a man out there who believed in "until death do us part" who would accept her son as his own. She was definitely keeping her options open for the right one. When an older woman walked in on her staring into the bathroom mirror, Robyn dismissed further musings. After all, she had tables to serve.

"Rob…" Doris, the head hostess, said, catching her strolling out of the ladies' room.

She hated that nickname. There was nothing masculine about her. She wasn't even a tomboy growing up, but she wasn't going to be petty. "Yes?"

"I just seated two in a booth in section four. One is a cutie pie. The other is hot. Sizzlin'." She fanned herself. "Whew!"

Right. As long as they left a big tip, that was all she cared about. With sixteen shopping days before Christmas, the crowd was taking advantage of the weather that hadn't delivered any ice or snow yet. She had three more hours to stand on her feet, and despite the top-of-the-line walking shoes, her back was aching. Straightening her shoulders, Robyn took a deep breath and made a beeline to the booth. She almost stumbled when she looked at the patrons.

"Hi, Mommy." Tyler grinned and waved.

Recovering from the surprise, Robyn gave her son a warm smile before squinting at her ex. "Derek, why are you here?"

"To get something to eat." He smirked.

*Oooh.* She didn't have time for his sarcasm. Showing up at their places of employment was off limits per their divorce decree, so why was he crossing the line?

"May we have our menus, Miss…Miss…?" His eyes sparkled with mirth as he snapped his fingers as if he didn't know her name. At one time, she had fallen in love with his playful nature. As their marriage deteriorated, his teasing just annoyed her.

"Humph, like you don't know it's Miss for now." She slapped his menu in front of him, then reached into her apron for a kids' menu and gently placed it with some crayons in front of her son. "Here, sweetie."

Derek leaned forward and whispered, "Be nice. You don't want to mess up your tip."

Why was she letting this man bait her? Lifting her chin, she put on a happy face and rambled off the specials as if he was an unknown patron. "Hi. My name is Robyn. Welcome to Red Lobster. Can I start you off with a fruit smoothie, raspberry lemonade, or Boston Iced Tea?" If left up to her son, he would order tea—he wasn't going to get it. She continued her spiel, "How about I get you started with our sampler?"

"Mommy, can I have popcorn shrimp and macaroni and cheese."

She gave Tyler a stern look.

"Please." He was a carbon copy of his father when he grinned.

"Sure, sweetheart." She faced Derek. "And you, sir?"

Tyler giggled. "He's Daddy, Mommy."

"Umm-hmm. I'll get your drinks and come back for your order."

"Hey," Derek said. "You don't know what I want."

"Trust me, I do." Robyn twisted her mouth and turned around. As she walked away, she heard Derek say, "You have a pretty mommy."

"Uh-huh. You should marry Mommy."

"I already did."

Her heart dropped. Why couldn't they have made it? Her parents had married for life. She thought she and Derek would follow in their footsteps, but after the first year of bliss, they couldn't agree on anything. Small disagreements turned into major arguments. She shook off the memories as she walked to the drink station.

She poured milk for her son, then a glass of water with a slice of lemon for his father. Derek's eating habits were predictable—or they used to be. He didn't like soda or juices. Health conscious, he preferred water. Returning to the table, she placed their glasses on it, then pulled straws out of her apron pocket.

"Mommy, I wanted a soda." He twisted his mouth and scratched his head.

"Milk will help you grow up to be strong and handsome."

"Like my daddy?" His hopeful expression was amusing.

Anchoring his elbow on the table, Derek rested his chin in the palm of his hand. He seemed to be anxious for her to answer.

"Like my daddy—your grandpa." She patted her chest, then turned to Derek with a smirk of her own. "So, have you decided, sir?"

When he toyed with the silky strands on his mustache, she knew he was stalling. She excused herself to check on her other customers. Spending too much time at one table could compromise her tips, so once again, she chose for him, and placed their orders.

She reappeared to bring them a basket of biscuits. With two demanding tables, Robyn hustled to please the patrons. In her peripheral vision, she saw a backup server going in the direction of her son's table.

This was the most she had seen of her ex in one day, and it unnerved her.

Derek wasn't the only man in the place who had an appreciative eye on Robyn Washington. He had watched for the last hour. At least, she still carried his last name, but for how long? He pledged her happily-ever-after. Would another man be able to succeed where he had failed? *Lord, I messed up.* He didn't want to think about it. He yearned for her attention so he lifted his hand.

"Yes," she said professionally with a blank expression. "Would you like a to-go box," she stated in a tone that wasn't meant to be a question.

"Actually, I would like to see a dessert menu." He grinned, hoping it would soften her heart like it used to. It didn't.

"It's in front of you." She lifted an eyebrow.

"Mommy, can I have a brownie?" Tyler's eyes drooped. The ice skating had worn him out.

She leaned forward. "You can have some pudding. It's too late for chocolate. Okay?"

"O-okay." He pouted. Clearly, he wasn't happy with his mother's decision. Neither was Derek when she walked away.

Derek had to get his son to bed, otherwise, he would have stayed until closing. Minutes later, he signaled for Robyn.

Flustered she returned to his table. "Yes, sir?"

He handed over his credit card. She didn't even look at him, and within minutes, returned. "I hope you enjoyed dining with us at Red Lobster."

*Enjoyed?* How could he, knowing the mother of his child was working two jobs as if he wasn't giving her enough to survive? Plus, she earned a good salary. If she was managing her money, she wouldn't need this gig.

"Daddy, I'm sleepy," Tyler whined and rubbed his eyes.

"Okay, buddy. Let's go home." He stood and heaved his son over his shoulder, then he reached in his pocket and pulled out a fifty-dollar bill. Instead of laying it on the table, he went in search of Robyn.

She was at the table where four men were flirting shamelessly as they placed their orders.

"Excuse me. You were a great waitress." He placed the bill in her hand and his son waved.

"Bye, Mommy."

He smirked. Yeah, let them know that she didn't need any more men in her life. *Thanks, son, for the backup.*

She kissed Tyler's cheek then faced her customers who seemed stunned. Turning on his heel, Derek walked away with more pep in his step. Checkmate, gentlemen.

# CHAPTER TWO

Why had Derek been in Robyn's dreams when she woke on Saturday morning? It had to be because he gave her the biggest tip of the night. She stretched her arms but didn't get out the bed. Or maybe it was the father-and-son image that stayed with her long after they had left. She smiled.

It was a maternal instinct to kiss him good night. It was comical the way her little boy, or maybe it was Derek's presence, which wasn't funny, but their action had shut down the flirts from her male customers at the table she was tending and possibly hurt her tips. Who cared? That was her little boy.

Derek had never been the jealous type. Neither was she when other women flaunted themselves when they were out, but people change.

Her ex's motives didn't matter. She and her son were a package deal, so if a man wanted to pursue her, he would have to accept Derek's involvement in Tyler's life.

Rolling over, she reached for her phone to call her best friend. Unlike her, Erica married a year after Robyn and was still with her husband. "Hey, Justin. Is your wife busy?"

He chuckled. "If she was, she would stop to talk to you and let me starve waiting for my eggs."

"Stop teasing her," Erica fussed in the background, then came on the line. "Hey, hard-working girl. What's up?"

"Derek Washington," she stated as she glanced around the bedroom they'd once shared. Since his departure, she'd totally revamped it—wall color, furniture, and decor. It was her attempt at erasing the passion they'd shared, and learning to be content sleeping alone.

"What did he do?" Erica sounded alarmed.

"Showed up at my house and job."

She exhaled. "Girl, you had me worried. Please tell me you two behaved in front of Tyler, and why did he come to your house?"

Robyn told her about her mother's rescheduled hair appointment, then added, "I hadn't seen him in a while."

"Still good-looking, huh?" Erica teased.

Robyn wished she hadn't noticed. "I'll give him that, but with hundreds of restaurants in the city, why did he have to come to Red Lobster and bring my baby?" Essentially, they had double-teamed her with their smiles.

"Was he a demanding customer? Did he cause a scene or leave without tipping?" her friend asked. "Two out of three is enough for me to put him on my do-not-like list."

"He didn't have any demands— just his presence was irritating. He couldn't make up his mind what to order though, but he did leave a big tip."

"Sweet," Erica said in a sing-song manner, which she probably capped with a grin. "If you two could have moved past your tit-for-tat spats, the Washingtons would still be married. Anyway, despite the divorce, I still believe you two love each other. Pastor quotes 1 Peter 4:8: *And above all things, love one another for charity shall cover the multitude of sins.* Translation: true love would overlook Mr. Washington's shortcomings."

"Well, we get along better from afar," Robyn insisted. Her life was drama-free without him.

"Although Christmas is about Christ reconciling the world of sinners to Himself, it's good for us to reconcile with each other, too," Erica said. Scriptures came second nature to her friend, and she didn't let Robyn slide when it came to reminding her about her Christian roots.

*I've had peace to give you all along,* God whispered.

Robyn knew that Scripture somewhere in John fourteen, but she had slacked off on her Bible study, so she couldn't recall the verse. Since she felt like she'd disappointed God after her divorce, she tried to keep Jesus at arm's length too. But at times, like right now, she still recognized His voice.

"Justin Williams, you're burning those eggs!" Erica fussed. "Girl, I've got to go. I guess you're going to have to pray to see what Derek is up to. Bye."

The challenge. That was her friend, always giving Robyn an excuse to pray. She didn't get out of bed right away. Instead, the quietness of her house caused her mind to drift.

She replayed the first of many arguments that led her and Derek to divorce court: the shouting, saying angry words they didn't mean—or maybe they did—then the separate bedrooms.

*Derek's nostrils flared as well as his biceps when he crossed his arms. How could a man look so handsome and mad at the same time?*

*"You can't keep going shopping behind my back. We're supposed to be saving."*

*She had ignored his bad attitude. "How could it be behind your back when I left you the receipts to balance the checkbook?"*

*"This is not funny, Robyn. We're supposed to be saving."*

*"We are saving—"*

*"No," he said, cutting her off, "I'm saving and you're spending."*

*"I've always been a bargain shopper. My mother taught me how to pinch pennies. I caught sales, and this stuff is for our new house."*

*"There won't be a house if you don't stay away from the malls. You can't go shopping with Erica every time she calls..." he shouted.*

Derek had made two mistakes that day, raising his voice and calling out her friend who loved him like a brother. Even now, Erica prayed that God would mend their hearts.

*Shocked by his attitude, Robyn had roared back, "You're not my daddy."*

*"But I'm your husband, and you're supposed to submit to and obey me."*

*"Obey you? I thought I was supposed to love you." Putting her fist on her hip, she rolled her eyes, then squinted. "It's easy to respect and obey a man who gives the same thing back. I'm a grown woman, not a child. My fathers, God and James Gibson,*

*wouldn't appreciate you treating me this way."*

They didn't speak for days, and that's when their parents intervened. Mrs. Washington gave him a tongue-lashing about how to treat the woman he loved.

Her mother didn't bite her words, either.

*"You're plain spoiled when it comes to money. Learn to save more than you spend." She frowned. "Now, as for Derek, my son-in-law needs a spanking for raising his voice at you. I'm sure Lane will take care of him. The greatest gift God gave a husband and his wife is the bedroom where the soft kisses, sweet words, and gentle touches can settle disagreements in love. That's why the Bible says in Hebrews 13:4 to keep the marriage bed pure, undefiled."*

*Sex on her mother's lips made Robyn blush. She lowered her lashes and fumbled with her fingers. "I do miss him."*

*"Then go home to your husband. Marriage is work. Be friends and lovers. Two is better than one. I'm reminded of that Scripture in Ecclesiastes, chapter four every day since your daddy passed away. You have a good man. He's rough around the edges, so pray for him and yourself."*

Then her mother prayed for her, kissed her on the cheek, and shooed her out the door.

Not long after, she and Derek not only kissed and made up, Robyn found herself expecting. With a baby on the way and the adorable outfits on sale, she had prayed for wisdom about her spending habits and God answered.

The first two years of Tyler's life were blissful. When she approached him about another baby, Derek broke her heart, adamantly stating, "Tyler is expensive enough. We can't afford any more."

Robyn had gone ballistic with that news. He knew she wanted more children, being an only child. Their communication broke down. Then she learned the company he had worked at for five years was about to close.

*"You could have told me. I needed to know that. I just went Christmas shopping. I can work more hours."* She tried to come up with a solution.

*Somehow, her solution made him snap.* "I'm a man. I can take care of my responsibilities."

*"Responsibilities?"*

They'd argued until Tyler woke from his nap, crying. That night, there was no marriage bed as he took to the guest bedroom, but not before saying, "If

I'm not enough for you, then divorce me."

His words had stung.

*Hold your peace,* the Holy Spirit had warned her, but she refused to submit to His voice and released some choice words she couldn't take back.

Derek stood when Robyn spotted him in the lobby at Red Lobster. "I don't want to fight, not now or ever again," he pleaded. "I've been waiting for more than an hour, hoping to catch you on a break."

He knew his presence drew suspicion from her coworkers, but he was tired of communicating with her through that message board. Surely, they could talk face-to-face by now—he hoped, he prayed, and hoped some more.

She folded her arms and stared up at him as he towered over her by half a foot. Remnants of her perfume tickled his nostrils.

"It's about Tyler," he whispered, inching closer as others buzzed by them.

She gasped and her eyes misted. "What's wrong with my baby? Is he hurt?"

Derek encircled her wrist to quiet her. "Our son

is fine, physically. He's at my brother's house"—another Washington divorcee, only Marlon had full custody of his two little girls—"playing with my nieces." He and his brother had unwittingly become second generation divorcees.

"So, what is this about?" She exhaled and stepped back.

"He's been crying in his sleep for you." When she lowered her lashes, Derek recognized the sign that there was something she wasn't telling him, like when she'd spent too much money on a shopping spree. He pressed her. "You knew about this?"

She looked away before facing him again. "Sometimes, he whimpers for you, too."

"And you didn't tell me?" He kept his tone even. Despite the revelation, he wanted to build her trust, so they could talk about anything—again.

"We have joint custody. He sees both of us equally. What else can we do besides taking him to a child therapist?" She jutted her chin. How many times had he guided that soft chin to his lips for a kiss?

*But not now, Washington,* he chided himself, crossing his arms and then uncrossing them. With two strong-willed personalities, Robyn might misinterpret his mannerism as the beginning of an argument. That wasn't the case. "It's two weeks before Christmas and Tyler's sixth birthday. Even though he is supposed to be with me this year for Christmas, I'm willing to share my time with you. I don't want you to be without him. Let's show him that we're still a family."

Her eyes said thank you, her mouth said, "I'll think about it—"

He loved her feisty spirit, except at the moment. "Which I know you won't." He cataloged her features as if it were the first time he'd seen her at their church picnic eight years earlier. Despite the weariness under her eyes, not much could distract from her beauty.

"Listen, we tried the family thing when we were married and it didn't work. It will only hurt Tyler if we start bickering."

"This isn't about you or me. Surely, for our son's sake, we can act like a couple, at least until after Christmas."

"God, help me to put up with you for fourteen days. My break is over." She spun on her heel and walked away in her signature strut, but this time, it had a drag to it. She was tired. He forgot to ask her why she was working two jobs. If she was drowning in debt, he would gladly rescue her for a reward—

being a couple again, even if it were only for Christmas.

# CHAPTER THREE

*Husband and wife are one flesh,* God whispered in Derek's ear until he woke him.

Groaning, he buried his head under the pillows. Why was God taunting him with that passage in Genesis? "If I could erase the past and start over with Robyn, I would do things differently, but I can't." The damage had been done, and they both had moved on.

*Man permits divorce. That was not My plan from the beginning,* God spoke again. *Read Matthew 19:8.*

Removing himself from the temporary hiding place, Derek turned on his back and stared at the ceiling. He had scrutinized the "what-ifs," and when he saw Robyn, they flooded his head. Pretending to be a happy family for Christmas would only magnify his regret. "God, I can't undo this."

*No, you can't. I can heal the sick, raise the dead, and save souls. Nothing is impossible through Me.*

Derek knew those passages, but Jesus was kind of late on the scene.

*I'm never late!* The Lord's voice thundered, almost shaking the windows in his bedroom. *Lazarus is proof of My restoration power.*

Granted, when Derek walked away from his marriage, God was next. His church attendance was hit-or-miss, more miss if his mother didn't nag him. But some things in the Bible, a Christian would never forget, like John, chapter eleven. Jesus not only waited for Lazarus to die, but was good and dead four days until he raised him. Was there a lesson for him to learn about his divorce?

Although Derek didn't plan to go to church, he would read those Scriptures. Before he could throw back the covers and get his Bible, which served as a centerpiece on his dresser, Tyler knocked on his door, then pushed it open. He was still rubbing the sleep from his eyes.

"Daddy, I'm hungry."

"Okay, buddy. Let's make pancakes and then we'll go see Grandpa."

After freshening up his son, Derek began his daddy duty of feeding his "mini-me."

"I want you to come live with me and Momma," Tyler said out of nowhere while he waited patiently for his food.

"Don't you like hanging out with me here?" Derek poured Tyler a glass of milk and watched him thank God for his food.

After tearing off a piece of pancake, Tyler stuffed his mouth and tried to talk. Derek corrected him, then changed the subject.

Every other Sunday, Derek zig-zagged across St. Louis to make sure Tyler saw his grandparents before ending their visits at Robyn's mother's house. An hour or so after breakfast, they dressed to visit his father, a man whom he loved despite his father having an affair while being married to his mother. It was debatable who divorced whom, but Tyrone Washington was working on marriage number three.

"Hey, Pops," Derek greeted him with a handshake as he and Tyler walked through the door.

"How's my favorite son and grandson?" He reached down and lifted Tyler in his arms, held up his hand for a high-five, then released him once Tyler slapped his hand.

"Liar," Derek mumbled jokingly. His father said that to all four of his sons, but it was true Tyler was his only grandson. Walking into the house, Derek scanned the front rooms, which screamed for attention. Growing up, his mother's home was never in a disarray, even with four boys. When it came to chores and tidiness, Lane Washington didn't play.

Since his father and Janice had no children, what was their excuse? In wife number three's defense, Janice was a great cook, and without grandchildren of her own, she was crazy about Tyler, who called her Gran Gran.

His father took his seat in a recliner and pointed the remote to the flat screen, muting the commentators' predictions on the Kansas City Chiefs match-up with the Denver Broncos. It was sure to be a good game, so what was he doing?

"How's Robyn?" his father asked without taking his eyes off the screen.

Crossing his ankles, Derek stretched his arms. "She's working a second job."

Whipping his head around, Tyrone's nostrils flared. "What? You're not paying your child—"

"Yes, Dad, and the house note, too."

He grunted and relaxed. "Good to hear." He was quiet as he stared in space. "I wish I had been a better role model for you boys when it came to marriage. I'd hoped you wouldn't take after your old man and be so quick to divorce."

When it came to cheating, Derek didn't inherit that gene.

"Maybe there's hope for your two younger brothers. They don't seem to be in a rush to tie the knot. Now, Marlon," he paused, shaking his head, "had no choice."

Derek agreed. His oldest brother thought he had a perfect marriage with two beautiful daughters. That was before he learned his wife had an affair. To even the score, Marlon had several. The sexual exploits led to his ex trying to kill him. She ended up in jail; his brother had the girls. At least there was never any violence between him and Robyn. If there had been, Derek would have restrained himself like Marlon. Yolanda took his brother's refusal to hit back as a sign of weakness and upped the stakes of violence by purchasing a gun.

"She was a good wife," his father said of Robyn. "You two didn't give each other enough time."

Derek sighed. "Time I can't get back," he murmured. "Believe me, I didn't go into marriage thinking about divorce as a way out, but I guess it was for the best since we stressed each other out."

Peeping around the corner, they both watched Janice giving Tyler a snack, then his father leaned forward. "To be honest, if I could do it all again, I would have stayed faithful to your mother. Leslie wasn't worth the affair," he said of his second wife in a hushed voice. They'd divorced after three years. Derek couldn't see his father's attraction or compatibility with his current wife of thirteen-plus years. Maybe they were together because Tyrone didn't want to be alone.

Would this be him in thirty or forty years, married to any woman so he wouldn't grow old without a companion? Derek shivered at the thought. "Dad, what's done is done. Isn't that what you've always told me?"

"Yeah." He unmuted the television and instantly they were drawn into the pre-game analysis.

The game ended with the Chiefs' winning touchdown. Derek bundled up Tyler, said his goodbyes, and headed across town for his mother's house in University City. Lane Washington was a stunning beauty when she was younger. All his friends had a crush on her. Robyn reminded him of his mother in a way—strong, independent, and pretty. He never asked his mother why she'd never remarried after her husband's betrayal. Once they arrived at her house, Derek used his key to let himself in.

"Grandma! Grandma!" Tyler raced to her and squeezed her leg with a hug. When she asked for a kiss, his son turned his cheek for her to deliver it to him instead of the other way around.

Derek chuckled. They ate and talked in codes about what she had gotten Tyler for Christmas. Too soon, it was time to drop his son off at his other grandmother's house, officially marking the end of his weekend visitation privileges.

"Tell Sara hello for me, and I'll give her a call soon."

The mothers-in-law were both church-going, Bible-toting Christian women. They could chase the devil away with their prayer meetings. When his and Robyn's marriage fell apart, they were so upset, they acted as if they had missed the rapture. Every time he thought they had gotten over it, they would remind him of their disappointments.

Half an hour later, he arrived at his former mother-in-law's home. He gathered his son's backpack and made the short walk to hand over his greatest accomplishment.

"Hi, Mrs. Gibson. Right on time." Derek tapped his watch as she opened the door before he made it to the porch.

"Shoo." She waved her hand. "A father is supposed to spend as much time as he can with his son. Children grow up too fast and go away."

"Thank you." He hugged the mature version of his ex-wife. "I found out Robyn has a second job," he said, hoping to get some insight as to why.

"Yep." She didn't bat an eye.

He waited for more. "You're not going to tell me anything, are you?" He tried a puppy-dog look.

"Nope." She didn't crack a smile. She loved him like a son, but when it came to her only daughter, Mrs. Gibson's allegiance didn't wavier.

Christmas was coming quickly whether Robyn was ready or not. She might not be a regular churchgoer, but she still had the fear of God to pray in the morning and at night, so on her knees she thanked Jesus for all things.

After she ate something light for breakfast, she began her task of toting boxes filled with decorations from the basement to the living room. Gritting her teeth, she dragged the last oblong box with the artificial tree up the stairs. She wanted it up before Tyler returned home.

Robyn assembled the branches in the appropriate spots. "What's the point?" she mumbled, knowing Christmas wouldn't be the same without Tyler with her. Plus, it was his birthday. Her heart pricked, and she felt the sting.

With her legs crossed, she rested her back against the sofa. Derek did have a solution, but they hadn't been together as a family in two years. Would he expect her to extend an offer him as the same courtesy when she had Tyler the following year?

His generous spirit was what drew her to him many years ago at their church picnic. That had been the first time their paths crossed in a congregation of a thousand-plus members.

Derek was assisting at the grill while she and Erica had signed up for babysitting duty on the playground.

*"I love children."* Robyn *sighed in awe of the little ones' antics on the slide.*

*"Whenever I get married, I only want one,"* Erica *said as she helped twirl one end of the jump rope for two six-year-olds.*

*"I was an only child. I would like to have three. And I want them two years apart..."*

Robyn didn't realize her eyes had watered until she blinked. Marrying the wrong man had made her miss her chance at those three children two years apart. Tyler would be six on Christmas Day. The best she could do was to give him stepbrothers or - sisters.

Pulling her legs up to her chest, she rested her head on her knees, closed her eyes, and let her mind continue to drift. Once the next shift of babysitters had reported for duty at the church picnic, she and Erica had made a beeline for the drink table. She could feel someone watching her. Looking over her shoulder, Robyn stared into the eyes of a brother wearing a black polo shirt that stretched across his chest to accommodate his bulging muscles. A white apron tied around his waist was smeared with barbecue sauce. When he smiled at her, their immediate attraction couldn't be denied.

He left his post and introduced himself as Derek Washington. Their love story was more than a summer fling. The following January, they were married, and Robyn enjoyed wedding bliss as the new Mrs. Derek Washington. Then, their personalities and opinions began to clash over simple things like shopping, savings, and where they should buy their first house. It was culture shock for Robyn that Derek didn't just go with the flow as her father had done with her mother.

Instead of three children two years apart, she had gotten married at twenty-three, had Tyler at twenty-five, and was divorced by twenty-nine. Now she was thirty-one and hoped for a second chance at love. Granted, she would take responsibility for some of their spats.

In hindsight, she did master money management. Because of those skills, Robyn was confident she could always provide for her son, even as a single parent.

Robyn didn't like pity parties, but when Tyler was away, she found herself attending them more often in her head. "Enough!" She stood and topped off the tree with lights. Before leaving for her second job, she wrapped gifts for her mother, Derek's parents, and Tyler, then placed them under the tree. Now, her house was starting to look more like Christmas.

Later that night, when Robyn ended her shift at the restaurant, she was glad working seven days in a row was only temporary. With sleep on her mind, Robyn thought she was hallucinating. Derek was there in the lobby—again.

Fuming, she marched up to him and came within inches of his face. "Do I have to file an order of protection to get rid of you? I have witnesses that I'm being stalked."

He handed her a bouquet of flowers that she hadn't seen him holding. She didn't accept them. "Do you have a few minutes?"

She rolled her eyes. "No, I don't. I'm tired. I

have to work tomorrow…"

"I'll be quick. If you don't mind me walking you to your car, we can chat on the way."

"Whatever." She snatched the flowers—her weakness—plus it didn't make sense to let God's beauty go to waste. She inhaled the fragrance and walked past him. "Let's go."

"First, let me say I'm sorry. I know it's long overdue, but I'm sorry for being a jerk and a bad husband."

Robyn swallowed and slowed her steps. She hadn't expected that. It got to a point in their marriage that "sorry" was erased from their vocabularies because neither refused to bend. She felt compelled to apologize, too, but she maintained her stubbornness.

When he had her heart, Derek broke it. "Accepted." She continued walking. Feet away from her car, she deactivated the alarm. He out-stepped her to open the door.

Another perk she missed: his chivalry. When they weren't arguing, her ex pampered her. Robyn threw her purse on the passenger seat before gently placing her flowers on top, then slid behind the wheel. When she reached to close the door, Derek held it firm.

"Wait."

She sighed. "You asked for a few minutes and you wasted them on the parking lot. I do have a full-time job to work in the morning."

"Why didn't you take back your maiden name when we divorced?"

"Huh?" He came up to Red Lobster to ask her that? He could have posted his question on their message board. Robyn blinked, then shrugged. "Because I did it God's way, waited until I married before I slept with a man and became a mother. I carry the name for my son's sake. When I remarry, I'll have a new name and hopefully, my husband will adopt-"

The fury on Derek's face came from nowhere. "My son is a Washington! I'll fight the courts if they try to terminate my parental rights. Tyler will not carry another man's surname nor will another man be his daddy!"

The same old Derek. He asked a question, didn't like the answer, and wanted to argue. "Good night." She snatched her door shut, started the ignition, and drove away.

She looked back in her rearview mirror. Derek had stuffed his hands in his pockets and dropped his head as if he were looking for loose change on the ground.

Humph. She gripped the wheel tighter. If her ex thought she would remain single for life, then he'd better step back. Robyn wanted to marry, and maybe it was time she went back to church and asked God for another husband. Clearly, her choice wasn't the right one.

# CHAPTER FOUR

Monday morning, Robyn's mother greeted her in the kitchen with a cup of coffee and a kiss. Since taking the second job, Tyler slept overnight on Sundays at his granny's house. So did Robyn. That way, she wouldn't have to wake him to go home.

"Thanks." She took a sip, then kissed her son who was crunching on his favorite cereal before joining him at the table.

"Hi, Mommy."

She spied the roses from the night before. Her mother had put them in water this morning and her eyes twinkled with mischief. "Flowers from an admirer?"

"I wouldn't call him that." She mouthed Derek's name in front of Tyler.

Her mother perked up. "He says you're working too hard, and he's concerned."

She huffed. "That man has no say over what I do."

Sara cleared her throat. "Grandson, go upstairs and get your backpack so you'll be ready to go." Dropping his spoon in the near-empty bowl, he did as he was told.

Once they were alone, her mother whispered, "Derek told me about Tyler crying in his sleep when he's away from his other parent." Alarm was etched on her face.

Robyn was silent. She was concerned about that, too. "He suggested doing things together as a family with him until Christmas may ease his anxiety."

Her mother physically relaxed. "I love the idea!"

"You would." She twisted her lips, then took another sip. "But the family thing didn't work for us."

"Because neither of you really invested the time to work at being a family. Couples give up on each other too easily," she fussed. "Stubbornness isn't a gift. Marriage is." She reached for a muffin and handed it to Robyn.

After giving thanks, Robyn took a bite. "He was the one who said the divorce word first." That cut her deep, so she retaliated and called his bluff. "I want a man who will fight for my love, not fight me on everything."

"Those were growing pains," her mother argued.

Without any siblings, they had a close relationship. Her mother listened patiently when she complained about Derek, but convinced her to try and work it out. But when she made up her mind about going through with the divorce, her resolve was too strong for even her mother to talk her out of it.

Robyn picked at the crumbs that fell to her plate. She wasn't happy about being a single parent, but at the moment, there was nothing she could do about it. She told the judge their marriage was irrevocably broken and couldn't be fixed, despite their vows to marry for life until death they would part. "This weekend gave me a glimpse at a picture perfect family." She sighed. "I wanted that."

"It's not too late, sweetie." Her mother's soft words gave her hope. "You have to admit, Derek is as handsome as ever, kind, and romantic. Rededicating your lives to Christ and rededicating your lives to each other will be easy." She giggled and eyed the flowers.

"We've moved on, remember?"

"Have you? Not without forgiving each other. The seventy times seven rule in Matthew eighteen applies to spouses."

"Ex-spouse," she corrected. "I have foresight into what a marriage with Derek is like."

"There were more good times than bad. Tyler is

proof of that."

Robyn sat quietly as her mother recalled one Scripture after another. The truth was, the flowers did melt away some resistance, but she was scared of getting hurt again. Derek's father had been married three times! Would her ex repeat the same pattern?

Enough talk about the man. Out of sight, out of mind. Things were back to their normal schedule this week anyway. Derek would pick up Tyler from kindergarten Tuesday and Thursday and drop him off at her mother's. End of story. She checked the time on the microwave. "I'd better get going." They stood and hugged as Tyler ran into the room with his things.

"I'm ready."

After zipping up his jacket and tying the hood under his chin, she slipped on her coat. They were heading to the door when her mother's phone rang.

"Good morning, Lane. How was your weekend?" She waved them goodbye and dismissed them to chat on the phone. "Of course, we can do lunch tomorrow..."

The mothers-in-law getting together. Yep, things were back to normal.

Derek's ex-wife was a tease, and she didn't know it. Everything about Robyn was soft and feminine—her inquisitive brown eyes, her pointy chin, and healthy hair. All that was accented by her sassy mouth, which he enjoyed kissing. Derek smiled at the memories of seeing her this past weekend, reminding him of her curves.

He had to bring his reminiscing to a halt. As a quality improvement manager for a health insurance company, he made good money, but the new job had come too late in his marriage to salvage their earlier financial problems.

By mid-morning, Mrs. Gibson's ringtone chimed on his phone as he was about to explain accreditation standards to a new member on his team. He excused himself to answer.

"Hi, Derek, I hope I won't be inconveniencing you today, but I won't be home in time to receive my grandbaby. I'm going to be tied up with this Christmas bazaar longer than I expected. Do you mind dropping him off at his house instead?"

*Mind? Are you kidding me?* He withheld his excitement. He should be thanking her for giving him a reason to see his ex again. "It's no problem as long as Robyn knows to expect me."

"She will. Thank you, son." She sounded

relieved as they said their goodbyes.

Hours later, he performed his Tuesday daddy duty and picked up Tyler. It seemed like he never had enough time with his little boy, although the judge made sure he and Robyn had equal custody.

While eating dinner at McDonald's, he listened attentively as his son talked about his playmates and the Christmas decorations they were making. As Tyler played with the toy included in his Happy Meal, Derek caught glimpses of Robyn in his expression. Tyler might be his carbon copy, but his mother's stubborn personality came through more times than not.

*Robyn.* She loved shoes and flowers. Stroking his chin, he came up with an idea. If a woman couldn't have too many shoes, then surely the same applied to flowers. "Want to take Mommy a present?" he asked once they finished eating.

"A toy?" Tyler's eyes were bright with hope as they got ready to leave. "No. How about pretty flowers?" Derek grinned as he made sure Tyler was secure in his car's booster seat.

His son frowned. "It's not a toy. She can't play with flowers." He shook his head. "I don't think she's going to like flowers."

*So little you know about your mother,* he

thought. "Trust me." He drove to the closest florist, and they went inside.

"It smells like Mommy in here," Tyler said after taking a deep breath.

Derek and the saleswoman chuckled. "See anything she would like, buddy?"

Tyler took off in the direction of a plant basket that was decorated with Santas and reindeers.

Definitely not what he had in mind. "No, son—flowers." Taking his small hand, they strolled throughout the showroom.

"I like that one, Daddy. It looks like my crayons." He pointed to a bunch of orange poppies.

"Umm-hmm." He was thinking something more upscale, sophisticated, and romantic as he spotted white calla lilies. They were sleek, delicate, and reminded him of Robyn. "What about these?"

Tyler shook his head and turned back to the poppies. "I like those."

The saleswoman smirked while Derek groaned. "I guess I'll take both."

Minutes later, they were en route to Robyn's house. Tyler was holding on to his flowers for dear life. He loved that little boy and would always be grateful to Robyn for giving him a son. His feelings for her that he thought were dormant were beginning to resurface.

While waiting at a stoplight, his cell rang through his Bluetooth radio.

Seconds after he answered, Robyn's sultry voice filled his car.

"Hi, Mommy! I got—"

Derek hushed him.

"Hi, baby." Her voice was magnified through the speakers. "Mom called and told me what happened. I'm home, so if it's not too much trouble, can you bring him now?"

Her voice sounded so sweet. "Nothing is too much trouble for my family."

She was quiet. Derek thought she had disconnected. "Okay. See you soon."

"Bye, Mommy!"

"Bye, Mommy," Derek mimicked and got a laugh out of her before the disconnection.

Fifteen minutes later, he parked in front of her house and debated if he was pushing his luck with her, even with a peace offering.

Robyn stood in the doorway.

After unstrapping Tyler from his booster seat, he handed him the calla lilies. "Give these to Mommy for me."

"Okay." Tyler raced out of the car toward the porch with his backpack barely hanging off his shoulder.

She opened the storm door for him, then squatted to receive the flowers. After what appeared to be her examining both bouquets, she took a whiff, stood, and glanced outside. His heart pounded. What was she thinking? If he could look into her eyes, he could take a guess.

She sniffed his lilies again, tilted her head, and waved like a beauty contestant who was just crowned. He waved back, then she slowly closed the door.

One day, if she ever opened the door to her heart to him again, God help him never to let it close. Yeah, a woman could never have enough flowers. Grinning, he drove home, praying for another opportunity.

# CHAPTER FIVE

Robyn's boss granted her an extended lunch break, so she called Erica to meet her at West County Center Mall to do more Christmas shopping. Plus, she wanted to get her friend's take on what Derek might be up to.

As she waited for Erica's arrival, Robyn window-shopped, back-tracking to a home decor store.

"Ho, ho, ho Hallelujah Christmas." Her friend's corny attempt at fusing together a commercial and religious holiday failed as she snuck up behind Robyn.

They laughed and hugged. A hat person, Erica wore a fashionable cap that was made of faux-fur and a trendy jacket that looked more like a vest with the sleeves out. It was a style Robyn never could figure out.

"I saw something in here I want to check out." Erica nodded and followed her inside as she gave her an update on her ex's shenanigans. "I don't know what to do about Derek. He's been bringing me flowers."

"You put them in a vase and add water." She did

a mock demonstration next to a tall glass cylinder that could be decorated with anything.

Robyn swatted her arm. "I'm talking about my ex."

"Then, maybe, you should talk to him," Erica stated as if she wasn't surprised by his gestures.

"You're no help." Robyn weaved around tables loaded down with knickknacks to follow her friend.

"I am helping, and you'll get my bill via PayPal to prove it." Erica picked up a figurine and checked the price before putting it back. "It's Christmastime, the season of giving. Stop thinking he has an agenda."

"He does. Derek wants us to do things with Tyler together until Christmas."

Erica spun around and wiggled her eyebrows. "Excellent. That would make a great gift that doesn't need unwrapping."

"Don't go there, girl. Christmas is about peace on Earth, and our divorce was the only way we could sign a peace treaty."

Taking a seat on a rose-colored Victorian love seat, Erica patted the space for Robyn to join her. "Two years is a long time to be on probation. Derek has proven to make good decisions concerning

Tyler. Stop trying to get free counseling sessions with me. Christmas is what, ten days away? Go with the flow."

"Fine." Robyn gritted her teeth and stood. If Erica wasn't such a good friend, she would accuse her of being biased, but her friend always had her back, whether she agreed with Robyn's decisions are not.

Her mind wandered as they combed through the store's merchandise, hunting for bargains. Finally, Erica dragged her out of the place in favor of following the aroma coming from the nearby food court.

As they stared at the Chick-fil-A menu board, Robyn sensed a presence before a deep voice whispered in her ear, "It's on the house."

Recognizing the person who made her shiver, she slowly turned to meet Derek's eyes. They were so close, they could have kissed. Robyn stepped back and swallowed. Whether she wanted to acknowledge it or not, he was made to wear suits and ties. In effect, he became gourmet eye candy.

They watched each other until Erica called his name a couple of times. He blinked first, then she did.

"It's been a while." Erica exchanged hugs as

Robyn and the two guys with Derek watched. They had to be his coworkers, since she had met one of the men once before her divorce; the other was unknown. It appeared they were also on their lunch break, but it was an annoying coincidence they happened to be at the same mall at the same time. Robyn needed this man to be out of sight, and out of mind.

"Ladies," the tall, light-skinned man said, clearly wanting to make his presence known. "I'm Craig Saunders, IT manager at Rizen Corporation."

So he was a coworker. He was handsome if she was attracted to his hazel eyes. She wasn't. Plus Derek was the true standout.

"I'm Mrs. Williams," Erica spoke first. She flashed her ring finger, basically warning Craig she wasn't interested.

Seeming to get the message, Craig turned to Robyn. She glanced at Derek who wore a guarded expression. "I'm Robyn."

The man grinned—or maybe it was a smirk. Either way, it wasn't attractive. "Is that Miss or Mrs.?"

Did Derek flinch? She thought he was about to throw a punch or something. Without thinking, Robyn grabbed his hand. She needed him to set a good example for Tyler, even if their son wasn't there. "It depends on the day. At the moment, I'm Mrs. Washington, because I have a handsome son that looks just like him." She tilted her head toward her ex.

Craig seemed to retreat and Derek appeared to exhale. He leaned closer and brushed a kiss on her cheek. "I didn't deserve that courtesy, but thank you."

She stopped breathing. Did he just touch her? Did his lips make her skin tingle? She exhaled and felt faint. They watched each other as if waiting for the other's next move.

Finally, he broke the trance when he reached into his back pocket for his wallet.

"Ah, you don't have to pay." She just needed him to go away.

"Let him," Erica argued, then winked. "My hubby treats me all the time."

Seriously? She glared at her friend. "He's not my husband anymore, remember?"

"Hmm." She shrugged. "I momentarily forgot."

Derek opened his mouth as if he had something to add, but closed it. Good, because their relationship wasn't up for discussion. He cleared his throat. "I will never say anything to Mrs. Washington that I don't mean." He pulled out a twenty, placed it in her palm, then wrapped his hand around hers before letting go seconds later.

After they left, Erica removed her hat and began to fan herself. "Whew. That was a lot of male hormones up in here, and it appeared the strongest prevailed. Go, Team Derek."

Robyn was too much in a daze to tell her friend to be quiet. "I should have taken back my maiden name."

"It's not too late—unless you plan to use Washington again." She giggled, then stopped. "Okay, sorry." She put her arm around Robyn's shoulder and squeezed. "Seriously, from what I witnessed, I do think he's harmless."

Robyn wasn't so sure as they placed their orders. Derek's touch had paralyzed all her senses.

Once they received their meals on trays, she followed Erica to an empty seat. Her friend said grace, then took the first bite.

"I don't know if I can survive another broken heart," she whispered to herself as she reached for a fry.

Erica slapped her hand away as if the fries were

hers. Robyn frowned. "Excuse me. You said you didn't want any." After she took a sip of her drink, Erica eyed her. "From the male dominance thing that was going on, I think Mr. Washington wants to repair the cracks. Jealousy never looked so sexy."

"I know." Derek never looked, smelled, and swaggered so seductively.

*Lord, please hold me back from assaulting someone who is two inches shorter than me,* Derek thought as he walked ahead of his coworkers. He didn't know who he was mad at, the new hire, Craig, who had spotted Erica and Robyn through a thick crowd, or himself for his territorial reaction.

*Craig released a soft whistle at something or someone who caught his attention. He and Tillman looked in the direction Craig was headed, and Derek's jaw dropped.*

*"Hey, isn't that Robyn?" Tillman asked.*

*Craig stopped in his tracks and turned around. "Who's Robyn?"*

*"Derek's ex-wife." Tillman nudged Derek's shoulder. "She still looks good."*

An hour later back in his office, Derek closed

the door and prayed. "Lord, please forgive me," he whispered as he joined his hands and rested his forehead on them. "Robyn has to know I still love her—she has to."

*She does,* God whispered.

# CHAPTER SIX

On Monday morning, a week before Christmas, Robyn's mother dropped the bombshell. "You and Derek don't need my house as the go-between for Tyler anymore. You're both no longer the same bitter, stubborn, and angry couple you were when you separated a few years ago."

"D–Divorced," Robyn corrected, then groaned. Could she handle more contact with Derek? His kiss, his touch, his soulful eyes…fool me once, shame on me, fool me twice, well, that would be a shame.

"It will save you time and wear on your body, driving from work in the county to the city to get my grandbaby, and back home in the county," she rambled on.

"It works for me," Robyn lied. Not really with the second job. One more weekend and she would be done for the holidays. "I'll talk to Derek."

"No need." Her mother grinned. "I already have. It's a go if you're okay with it." Sara Gibson lifted an eyebrow. "Which I'm sure you will be."

She was in a good mood until it seemed like her mother was forcing her hand. That's all she needed was Derek at her door twice a week. Their close encounters the previous week had chipped away at the wall of protection she'd built around her senses. His words had hurt her and he couldn't take them back, even if he tried.

Her mind continued to drift at the office until she had to put aside a project from her boss to log onto TalkingParents.com.

Mom told me about the tentative arrangement. You'll have to feed Tyler and help him with homework because I won't be home until seven. Those were her late days since her boss visited with project managers at his two warehouses on those mornings.

Derek called. His greeting had a ring to it, and she imagined his smile. "Can we do away with the message board? I'd much rather hear your voice."

*I like hearing yours, too,* she admitted to herself only. "Okay, for now."

He chuckled. "See, we can do baby steps. Have you finished your Christmas shopping between working two jobs?"

Robyn squinted. Was he fishing for information? "Not yet, but I won't stop until I get every toy our baby wants." She paused. That was a first. She never referred to Tyler as *their* baby. He was always *her* son.

"I have a special gift for you," he cooed in her ear.

"Me?" She blinked in shock. More than the unexpected flowers? "Ah, we're supposed to exchange Tyler's visiting schedule, not gifts."

"What I want can't be purchased at a counter."

Her heart pounded as she waited for him to reveal what was on his wish list.

"All I want for Christmas is for us to spend time together. Every day for seven days, even if it's for thirty minutes."

She sighed, picked up a pen, and began to doodle on a note pad, calculating the number of hours she would be forced to be in Derek's presence.

"Robyn Shantelle Washington?"

She smiled at his use of her middle name. "Oh, okay, but I don't see how I can shop for our son—" she said "our" again "—without him seeing what I'm buying."

"I'll keep him distracted by helping him pick a gift for you. Our parents bought us things right under our noses and we didn't know it."

Against her better judgment, she agreed. They chatted a few more minutes until Derek was interrupted at work. "See you tomorrow, Mrs.

Washington."

Now, he was taking too much for granted. "It's Ms. Washington to you." What a way to start a work week.

Tuesday morning as Robyn dressed for the office, she took so much extra care in her appearance, going with bright, cheerful attire, even Tyler noticed.

"You look pretty, Mommy." He stared at her as if he hadn't seen her look her best before. Truth be told, it had been a while since she really cared about what she wore outside of her business attire.

She rewarded him with a kiss. "Thank you, baby." What would Derek think? *Who cares?* her voice of reason reminded her.

At work, her boss even commented. "You're glowing today. Did you change your makeup or something?"

*Men,* Robyn kept from rolling her eyes as she simply accepted the compliment. In all honesty, she actually focused on accenting her eyes and wore a dash of blush. Instead of her generic black, brown, and gray suits, she had opted for a festive multi-colored dress and a red blazer. "It's dinner and shopping, not a date," she kept telling herself throughout the day.

When she arrived home, Derek and Tyler were already there, sitting in the car, waiting for her.

Following her in the house, Derek stood larger than life in his black cashmere coat and hat. Unbuttoned, it exposed his dark suit minus a tie. Tucked under his arm was a white furry bear with a red rose.

Their son was also toting some kind of stuffed animal.

"For you," he whispered. Derek's eyes sparkled and a smile stretched the silky hairs on his thin mustache. He wore the same expression many years ago at the picnic, one that drew her into his love trap, but she had escaped, never to be snared again—she thought. She had to suck in her breath. Not good. His cologne was intoxicating.

"Daddy bought this for me!" Tyler held what looked like an alligator.

"I see."

While Tyler dumped his backpack on the bench in the hall, Derek didn't move from his spot as if he was waiting for her permission. He peeped into the living room. "Nice tree."

"Daddy doesn't have a Christmas tree," Tyler snitched, latching onto his father's hand, then dragging him farther into the living room.

"No, but I have presents for my boy."

Because they attended a Bible-based church during their marriage, the pastor advised parents not to dilute Christmas with Santa Claus. *"If we're going to celebrate Christmas, let's reserve it for Christ. We don't want to breed lies, myths, and fables to our children. Jesus is a God of truth."* She and Derek had wholeheartedly agreed. Even though she didn't attend church regularly anymore, his words had stayed with her.

"Yay." Tyler jumped in place, pulling her back to the present. "I'm hungry."

His choice was no surprise: McDonald's. Robyn tried to limit his fast-food visits to once a week in favor of home-cooked meals from her or her mother, but she didn't protest it. In the car, melancholy swept over Robyn as she strapped her son in his booster seat. This was one of many family outings she had assumed would always happen. It saddened her to the point her eyes misted, so she peered out the window and let the houses decorated with lights distract her.

Hunger was forgotten once Tyler entered the

restaurant and saw the playroom. "Ten minutes, young man, then you have to eat something before it gets too late," she told him.

Derek helped Tyler take off his coat, then assisted her with hers before they chose a table that kept their son in view.

"You look pretty."

There was something about that word that made Robyn blush. It sounded genuine when a man said a woman was pretty rather than gorgeous, beautiful, or stunning. "Thank you." She dismissed him and looked toward the playroom. Not only did she feel Derek's stare, but her peripheral vision confirmed he was watching her.

"You know, we can be friends," he said softly.

"We were friends, once," she stated without facing him. "I wound up marrying you, and you wound up divorcing me." She turned and gave him a pointed stare. She felt an argument brewing, and suddenly the family outing seemed like a bad idea.

But instead of challenging her, Derek bowed his head. "You're right. I knew I had a good woman and wife, but somehow, the devil blinded me. I cringe when I think about the things I said to my beautiful wife."

Hmm. Now it was a toss-up whether she was stunned more by his admission, or whether she liked him calling her beautiful. Her heart softened. "So, why did you? Your words hurt and forced me into a corner. I came out swinging."

He glanced away, then back at her. "I know. It's no excuse, but that's how my father settled a blow-up, threatening to leave. It was the norm during my childhood, and I guess I tried to follow in his footsteps. Like my father, I wanted to be the king of my castle and demand you submit to me." He paused and yelled for Tyler to be careful, then finished, "Recently, Dad said that walking away from my mother had been his biggest mistake." Regret seemed to sag his facial features.

Something made her reach across the table and rest her hand on top of his. "I had regrets, too. As an only child, I was spoiled and got everything I wanted. I brought that mindset into our marriage and I'm sorry." She exhaled, feeling lighter with her apology.

In response, he trapped her hand by placing his on top, then checked on their son.

Not one to easily admit when she was wrong when it came to him, she confessed, "The truth is, you were right about my spending habits." She offered a tentative smile.

"Do you need money? Is that why you're working two jobs. I'll do whatever I have to make sure you and Tyler are okay." The sincerity in his eyes backed up his statement.

"No." She shook her head and admitted, "Because of you, I've learned how to manage money. Thank you. My company cutback and the bonuses were the first things to go, which was my shopping money for Christmas. Since I didn't want to touch my savings, I took this gig for a month. It's only temporary."

"I'm in no position, nor do I have the right to make a demand, but please quit."

Squinting, Robyn took a breath as she could feel her attitude rising. "I make the decisions in my house and—"

"I said please," He said softly and held up his hands in surrender. "I'll match whatever you're making at Red Lobster."

She chuckled. "Ooh. You are setting yourself up for bankruptcy."

"Bankrupt me," he taunted and grinned, reminding her of their son. "I'm serious here. I'll write you a check to cover your bonus. I want you home with our son and...Christmas is five days away. You never answered about being a family for the holidays."

When the decorations came down, could she resurrect the wall around her heart? He mentioned baby steps earlier. "We are a family—living in separate homes."

"You and that sassy mouth..." He stared at her lips and then bit his own.

"I'm hungry," Tyler yelled, running toward them full steam.

While she braced for impact, Derek released her hand. He stood and hunched like a football player, then scooped up Tyler who squealed in delight.

She would never grow tired of watching the daddy side of her ex. They placed their orders, which included a Happy Meal, plus she made Tyler eat a side salad.

Between swallows, Tyler talked about his teacher and her puppy, which she'd brought to class. A couple of times, she caught Derek watching her. Not only did she wish she could read his mind, but she also wanted to know what he'd gotten her for Christmas. Her holiday presents were limited to her mother, Erica, her boss, and son. A man hadn't bought her a gift since their divorce.

Soon, Robyn checked her watch and announced it was Tyler's bedtime.

Her son groaned. "Can Daddy sleep at our house tonight?" he pleaded.

Robyn looked to Derek to intervene, but he seemed amused by the spot their son put her in. Great, make her the bad person. She took a deep breath. "Daddy likes sleeping at his own place."

"No, I don't," he teased, and she scowled.

Clearing her throat, she chose her words carefully. "Daddy has his own house, and we have ours. But your father is going to spend more time with us until your birthday." Had she actually agreed to Derek's request? Judging from the smirk on his face, she had.

"Come on." She stood and reached for her coat. Derek snatched it first and helped her slip it on. Looking over her shoulder to thank him, she was held hostage by his closeness. She stuttered, "Th– Thank you," before stepping back and regaining control. Day one down. She could only imagine what her attraction to Derek would be on day five.

# CHAPTER SEVEN

Christmas was coming too soon for Derek. Wooing his ex under the guise of family outings would end. He needed more time to win her over for a second chance at them being a real couple.

This evening had been a short excursion. They enjoyed a buffet dinner, then drove through Tilles Park for the annual Winter Wonderland Christmas lights village. Robyn *ooh*ed and *ahh*ed as much as his son at the gingerbread light display.

When he turned into Robyn's driveway, their son was dozing. Before getting out to open Robyn's door and gather Tyler, Derek took her hand. He could no longer be on good behavior. She responded with a curious expression. "Thank you for tonight."

She nodded with a smile as if she knew what he meant. Their being together was more about them as a genuine couple than a pretend couple for Tyler's sake. Love burst through his heart, and he wanted to wrap her in his arms and kiss her as if it were the first time. He wouldn't—not yet. Timing was everything, so Derek exhaled and stirred their son awake.

As the three approached the front door, he

noticed it was ajar. Immediately, he went into protection mode as Robyn gasped. "I want you and Tyler to get back into the car and call the police—now." He shoved Tyler into Robyn's arms.

"What's wrong, Daddy?"

"Go," he ordered.

"Stop trying to be a hero, Derek Washington. You're worth more to me alive than dead." The softness in her voice and the fear in her eyes made him pause. "Let's wait for the police together."

He sighed. "All right."

After taking their son back, Derek wrapped his arm around Robyn, then hurried them to safety. He kept an eye on the premises while she called 9-1-1. He might not have a weapon, but he had never lost a fight growing up with his fists.

The police arrived in four-and-a half minutes; Derek was counting. Once he explained who they were and the situation, two officers went inside with their weapons drawn.

"Daddy, why are the policemen coming to my house?"

He exchanged glances with Robyn before silently praying, *Lord, give me the words to say to my little boy so that he won't be afraid.* After five seconds and nothing, Derek accepted he had to fend for himself. "They want to make sure you and Mommy are okay."

"Why?"

"Because your door was open," he explained.

"But Mommy always locks the door. She taught me how," Tyler stated matter-of-factly, leaning toward the front seat.

A tall, thin officer walked back to the car. "All clear. Mr. and Mrs. Washington, I need you to come inside and identify if anything has been taken."

*Mr. and Mrs.?* It had been a long time since he'd heard that in one sentence. His eyes strayed to Robyn's hand and the missing wedding ring. *Where was it?* he wondered. Did she have it tucked away or did she sell it?

As they retraced their steps to the house, Robyn leaned on his shoulder. Wrapping his free arm around her, he wanted more than anything to be her hero in love. She snuggled closer. They walked in sync as they climbed the stairs and crossed the threshold.

"The presents." Robyn started shaking, and it seemed like her legs were about to buckle. Tightening his hold around her, he kept her steady.

She faced the officer and then him, "All the Christmas presents are gone." She broke away, flopped down on the nearby seat, and cried.

Tyler wailed, "My toys are gone, Daddy." He looked at him with pleading in his eyes as if he could fix it.

Derek took a deep breath and carried him to sit on the sofa next to Robyn. He did his best to console his family. "Those things are replaceable. You and Tyler aren't."

She nodded, but he doubted she believed him.

"Ma'am, sir," the officer said gently, "we need you to go through the house and see if anything else was taken."

Derek stood and reached for her hand. "Come on. I'll go with you."

A female officer coaxed Tyler to her side and showed him her badge. Intrigued, his son began to ask questions.

Linking his fingers through Robyn's, they started upstairs. The house seemed bigger when he lived there. Unless his son was messy, which Robyn wouldn't tolerate, the thief or thieves had ransacked his son's bedroom. He wanted to curse, but refrained from doing so. Not only because of Robyn but he knew God was listening, as well. Instead, he thanked the Lord that his family wasn't there.

When a tear trickled down her cheek, he smoothed it away. The next check was the master bedroom. Was it the same, or did she do a complete overhaul? His answer came when he walked in behind her.

What had she done with the expensive burgundy bedroom set she'd insisted on them having? They both had worked overtime to pay for it. Now, the walls were a lilac color, and all the furniture was white.

She made a beeline to her dresser and shuffled through her jewelry box, which was on its side. "My diamond earrings and wedding ring are gone!" She stomped her feet and balled her fists. "Crooks!" She hurried past him to the end of the hall.

Their old bedroom furniture was behind door number three. In the corner was a desk. If she had a computer, the thieves had swiped that too.

"I feel so violated! They've come in my house and our bedrooms!"

Gathering her in his arms, he hugged her as she sobbed softly. He released her only because he wanted her to look into his eyes when he made her an offer. "You can stay at my place. I'll take care of getting the locks changed and upgrading this old security system."

Her expression was unreadable as she shook her head. "Thanks, but I'll stay here. This is my home."

She didn't sound convincing, but he wouldn't pressure her, just yet. The more he reflected on their marriage, Derek realized some of their spats weren't worth the wasted minutes arguing. He nodded as he considered plan B. "Come on, let's tell them what else is missing."

The policewoman stood when they entered the living room. "You have a smart little boy."

Puffing out his chest, Derek grinned. "Yes, we do. Thank you."

They waited in the living room as the evidence team arrived, then dusted for fingerprints. After Derek turned on the faux fireplace, he sat next to Robyn and held his son tight as she rested her head on his shoulder. He pushed his liberty and kissed the top of her hair.

Closing his eyes, he whispered, "Thank You, Lord." Derek didn't want to think of what would have happened if Robyn and Tyler were home at the time of the break-in: rape, kidnapping, murder. He shivered, and she glanced up at him. Their eyes met, but neither said a word.

"Daddy, will you be here in the morning?" Tyler asked as his eyes drooped.

"Yes, son." He would protect his own.

When the evidence team was finished, Derek shifted to stand to speak with them outside the living room.

"It looks like there could have been two. One came through the front since you didn't have a lot of decorative lights outside like the other homes. Another one broke in the back door. I would suggest changing both locks. Here's the number to an emergency locksmith."

Thanking them, he accepted the business card, made the call, then returned to the sofa to cuddle with his family. Someone would be there soon.

Robyn stirred an hour later after the door locks had been changed. "Thank you." She covered a yawn. "It's late, so you'd better go." She didn't sound convincing; neither did she look certain of her request.

"I'm not leaving you two here by yourselves." Derek wasn't backing down or going anywhere. Because of their son, she wouldn't raise her voice in front of him, even if Tyler wasn't awake. "I can sleep here." He patted the thick cushions on the sofa.

"Not in my house as a single mother. I don't entertain sleepovers with men," she said with more defiance.

"I'm not any man. I'm the *father* of *our* son…" He wanted to profess his love.

"And my ex." She stood. Fire replaced fear in her eyes. "You have to leave now so we can get some sleep."

"You were sleeping until you woke up," he argued. She might not be scared, but he was afraid to leave them.

"Good night, Derek." She marched to the door and fumbled with the new locks before opening it.

He didn't move until she planted a fist on her shapely hip. Reluctantly, he walked out. She closed the door behind him and turned the lock before his feet landed on the third step.

Collapsing against her door, Robyn exhaled a couple of times. Although she was frightened, knowing she had been violated in her sanctuary, she was a single mother and had to be strong for her son.

*He that dwells in the secret place,* she heard the Lord Jesus' whisper.

How many times when she attended church had she quoted Psalm 91:1? *He that dwells in the secret place of the Most High shall abide under the shadow of the Almighty.*

Wrapping her arms around her frame, she glanced up the stairs. There was no way she would let her son see his room in its present condition. The hero worship he gave Derek didn't go unnoticed, but she had to prove to her son that Mommy could protect him too.

After turning off the lights on the tree, which was bare underneath of the twelve gifts she had purchased, she chanced a glance out the window and blinked. Derek's car was no longer in the driveway. Instead, he was parked in the front of her house. "Stubborn," she mumbled, but her heart corrected her, *No, that's love.*

It was true. Since Derek had shown up at her door last week, he'd made her feel loved. And because she still had feelings for him, she raced upstairs and grabbed a pillow and blanket out of the closet.

Back downstairs, she checked on Tyler, then slipped on her coat. She fumbled with the new locks again, quickly opened the door, and ran to the curb. Derek's arms were folded across his chest. His head was propped against the window and his lids fluttered, fighting sleep. Maybe, he was her hero. She banged on the window and startled him.

She giggled. "Here." When he unlocked the door, she opened it and threw the blanket and pillow at him, then hurried back to her house.

Next, she coaxed Tyler awake and guided him up the stairs to her bed. Once he was undressed and under her covers, she went to work on restoring his room before he woke.

Two hours later, she climbed in the bed, but not before peeping out the window one more time. Her eyes watered. The street light gave her a view of the man she had once vowed to love, and it dawned on her that despite their petty misunderstandings, her love for Derek Washington had rekindled. She was in big trouble.

# CHAPTER EIGHT

Friday morning, Robyn stirred after a series of pats on her back. "Mommy, you awake? Mommy."

It was two days before Christmas. Tyler's school was closed for break, and she was off from her day job until January second, so why was she being disturbed? She groaned, opened her eyes, and rolled over. She blinked until Tyler's face came into focus. Why was her son in her bed? Then the previous night's events came rushing back. She sprang up, dazed.

"Daddy's hungry."

"What? Your father's not here." She slid out of bed and raced to the window. Sure enough, Derek's car hadn't moved. She turned and frowned at her son. "How do you know he's hungry?"

"Because I want something to eat."

Like father, like son, both had hearty appetites. She shook her head. "Go wash up and brush your teeth."

Her plans had changed literally overnight. This would have been her last weekend at Red Lobster. She signed up to work when she thought Derek would have Tyler, but that was before the previous night. She freshened up, then called her mother.

The panic in her mother's voice was unmistakable. "Baby, are you okay? Was Derek with you?"

"Yes, but the thieves stole all the gifts, my jewelry, and Tyler's games." She had to remember to file a claim with her insurance adjuster. The jewelry alone was worth thousands. Derek might fuss about her spending habits, but when he spent money on her, he didn't see dollar signs.

"Stuff can be replaced. Christ gave us the greatest gift, which isn't replaceable."

After reassuring her mother that she was all right, Robyn hurried off the phone to cook breakfast. Not only was her son hungry, apparently, his father was too. "Tyler, how did you know your daddy was outside?"

"Because when I woke up, he wasn't here. I couldn't find him." Tyler's eyes widened with fear. "So, I called him, and he said to look out the window and he waved from the car." He grinned.

Smiling back, she rubbed his hair. "Put on your clothes and run outside to get him." She returned to the kitchen and began to boil water for the rice.

"I'm ready," Tyler said, taking as many steps as his legs would allow for him to reach the landing in record time.

She put on his coat and opened the door for him. Folding her arms, she leaned on the frame as her son ran to the car. He banged on the window.

"Daddy, Mommy says c'mon," he shouted.

Robyn chuckled and walked back to her kitchen and grabbed a half of dozen eggs from the refrigerator to scramble after pouring rice in the pot. Minutes later, she heard Derek's heavy footsteps approach from the hall. She spun around and laughed.

His eyes were swollen, his hair was in need of a brush, and the wrinkles in his suit wouldn't start a fashion trend. She laughed, then pouted, "Poor baby."

"Funny," he mumbled, shifting the pillow and blanket under his arm. "Do you have an extra toothbrush?"

"Hall closet along with soap, washcloth, and mouth rinse."

"Okay." He nodded. "Make fun of me if you want, but I clean up real good."

"Yes, I know," she mumbled under her breath

and turned back to her stove. For too short of a time, she woke up next to a hunk and was never disappointed. Even when they went to sleep angry in the marriage bed, they woke up in each other's arms.

Before long, Derek returned with Tyler by his side. Gone was the weariness and his wrinkled dress shirt. His T-shirt stretched over his chest. His eyes sparkled, knowing how much she appreciated his physique. She crooked her finger at him, and he began to approach.

"Yes." His deep voice seemed to echo as he towered over her.

"Thank you for staying last night. I did feel safer, knowing that you were close by."

He placed his strong hands on her shoulders and rubbed her arms. His touch put her in a hypnotic state. "I'm here to stay."

She blinked. "Not in this house."

He shook his head. "I'm talking about my heart." He reached into his pocket. What was he doing? She sucked in her breath when he retrieved a blue velvet bag with a drawstring. He opened it and pulled a necklace from it. "Sorry, it's not wrapped, but I'm giving you my heart." He patted his chest. "I'm trusting you with it."

She accepted it, speechless.

"We need to talk, Robyn. Really talk."

Her vision blurred as her mind flashed back two years earlier when the judge asked if their marriage could be saved. She and Derek vehemently said no. If asked at this moment, Robyn wouldn't be so quick to answer.

Her mind swiftly returned to the present. "Not today." Clearing her throat, she gave herself space to rationalize what she was doing. "I need to go shopping to replace those presents," she rambled on nervously.

"I'm inviting myself." He smirked, and she didn't argue. Truth be told, she liked him close by. It had to be because of the break-in. "First, I need to get a new security system installed here ASAP."

Once they were sitting at the table, Derek reached for their hands. Usually, she let Tyler say grace, but she didn't stop Derek as he bowed his head.

"Oh God, thank You. We have so much to be thankful for this morning. Thank You for watching over my family...and I thank You for giving me them." He paused. "I ask that You bless and sanctify this delicious meal my wif—she cooked—" he corrected, "and I'm asking for restoration in Jesus' name. Amen."

Robyn fluttered her lids slowly. While she processed the slip of his tongue, Tyler was the first to speak.

"I like when you to pray, Daddy." He grabbed a bacon strip and crunched on it, spilling bits on his plate.

"It was from the heart," he said, looking at her.

It didn't take long before Tyler started talking about his teacher's puppy—again. When she remembered the fruit salad in the refrigerator, she got up to get it.

"You have a pretty mommy, you know that?" Derek's whisper was loud enough for her to hear.

She smiled when her son agreed with an "uh-huh." That was the second time Derek had said she was pretty. Now she wondered what else he had said behind her back to their son.

Things hadn't worked out the way Derek had hoped. Instead of accompanying his beautiful ex-wife shopping, he stayed behind at the house he had built for them to oversee the installation of a new security system.

Once the installers had finished, Tyler coaxed him to his room where they played for hours until he began to rub his eyes.

"C'mon. Nap time."

"I'm not sleepy," Tyler slurred. "Tomorrow is my birthday and Jesus' too."

"I know." Derek chuckled. He stood and lifted his five-year-old for one more day in his arms, then carried him to bed.

As he was covering Tyler, his son asked, "You staying, Daddy?"

"Yeah." He winked. "I'll be here when you wake up." He turned to leave the room, but Tyler stopped him.

"I mean forever."

What did his son know about forever? Slipping his hands in his pockets, he nodded, hoping he could seal the deal, then walked downstairs.

Back in the living room, he surveyed the holiday decorations draped across the mantle and the tree. He sat on the sofa and imagined being part of this household again.

As he reminisced, he heard car doors slam. Laughter and chatter filled the air until the door opened. His three favorite ladies came in with their arms filled with bags.

When Robyn's mother told his mother about the burglary, both women showed up at the house. Lane Washington wasn't happy she didn't hear the news from him. Once they were convinced that all was well, they volunteered to go shopping with Robyn.

He jumped up and hurried to relieve them of their packages, planting kisses on their cheeks as he retrieved their loads. Robyn blushed while his mother and mother-in-law's eyes twinkled with mischief at his gesture.

"Did you leave anything at the store?" he joked.

"We tried not to," Mrs. Gibson said. "Besides, you know we like to give Tyler separate presents—for his birthday and Christmas. Where is my grandson, anyway?"

"Taking a nap," he answered but kept his eyes on his wife—forget the ex part. Their hearts were one. Otherwise, they would have moved on, right?

"Did the security people come?" Robyn asked casually as if she was unaware that his heart was speaking to hers.

"Lane, let's take this stuff into the kitchen and begin to wrap them—"

"No." Robyn waved her off. "I was going to do

that tonight."

"Nonsense, sweetie. We can do that. Why don't you entertain your guest?" She winked and ushered his mother to the kitchen.

Left alone, Derek stretched out his hand. After a slight hesitation, she took it, then he guided her around to the sofa. They sat facing each other.

"You think they're setting us up?" Derek grinned and tilted his head, waiting for her to answer.

"Probably, considering all they talked about was how heroic you were to watch the house all night from your cold car."

He chuckled.

"I kindly reminded them that you had a pillow and blanket and slept most of the night."

"I had one eye open," he said, defending his honor. Derek glanced over his shoulder to make sure their mothers weren't snooping around the corner. He took a deep breath and exhaled. Here it goes. "There is nothing about you I would change. I'm sorry I didn't know that before now."

She shifted in her seat, then lifted an eyebrow in a dead-on challenge.

He braced himself for her sass, but they needed

to speak from the heart.

"Nothing?" She smirked. "I thought there was plenty about me you wanted to change when we were married. Number one: obey your every command."

Derek flinched. He couldn't believe he had twisted the Word of God in his favor, but that had been learned behavior from watching his father and one of his brothers. Surrendering to Christ had been his way to break the cycle, but he had failed God, himself, and his wife. "I didn't deserve you back then. I wasn't mature enough to love you as a woman. God gave me the passage in Ephesians 5 recently."

He waited for her to come to his defense and say, "You weren't that bad," but she was silent, so he cleared his throat and proceeded, "Talk to me. Are you happy, because I'm not complete being a part-time dad and an ex-husband."

Robyn exhaled. She scanned the room as if debating what she would say, then she folded her arms. "Okay, here's my honesty. I don't like being a single mother. I want to be a wife in the good times and bad, not the fantasy of a perfect marriage. I can't think about dating without considering Tyler."

Derek studied her, trying to read between the

lines. "Are you saying you don't plan to remarry?" His heart pounded. If she said yes, did she mean with him? Or would he be the cause of her never being willing to step in the ring again.

"When the right man comes along. First, I need to return to God, and the next time around, I want to be a godly wife and have a godly husband."

"Do you think that could be us?" He reached for her hands and rubbed his thumbs against her soft skin.

"We have a history. Our son proves that, and I do love you, and I care." She pulled back from his touch. "I'm just not convinced *us* doing a repeat wouldn't have the same outcome."

*Ouch.* Was that statement based on his father's track record? Nah. *I got this.* "I can convince you." He grinned.

She shook her head. "That's not enough. I need for my heart to be in sync with the Lord Jesus again."

"Should we expect the Washingtons at Christmas service in the morning?" his mother asked, popping her head in the room.

He and Robyn exchanged knowing glances. Their mothers probably had been eavesdropping on them the whole time. He shrugged. "It has been a while. Plus, we can celebrate the holiday and Tyler's birthday after that."

Robyn exhaled and smiled while Derek wondered if this would be like old times, but only the good times in their marriage.

"Yes!" their mothers said in unison. "Then, carry on."

# CHAPTER NINE

"Hallelujah Chorus" stirred Robyn from her sleep on Christmas morning. She smiled, replaying the melody in her head. Sunshine filtered through her bedroom blinds, forcing her eyelids to flutter open. She took a deep breath, exhaled, but didn't get up as she processed what would take place that day. She realized she missed attending church and was keeping Tyler from building a relationship with Jesus.

*Don't keep your son from coming to Me for I have come this day to prepare My Kingdom, which is not on this Earth. That is My gift to anyone who comes to Me with the innocence of a child,* God whispered. *Read Matthew 19:14.*

Robyn immediately repented for cheating her son out of his godly blessings in favor of worldly gifts. She reflected on the part-time job she had taken so her son would have a Merry Christmas with clothes, games, and toys. After the break-in, she called her manager at Red Lobster and quit because she had compromised her priorities, but all that would change today.

She would allow Tyler to open one gift before

church and the others after that. She, Derek, and Tyler would go to service as a family—a family. Her eyes watered as she thought about the break-in again. She shivered with fear, then realized how God had orchestrated things for her and Tyler not to be home but with Derek.

*Though the devil intends evil against you, he did not succeed,* God reminded her.

Blinking back moisture from her eyes, she got out of bed and slid to her knees. She prayed and thanked Jesus for her blessings. Robyn barely said Amen when Tyler barreled into the room. "It's my birthday, Mommy. Happy birthday to me and Jesus!" He was about to jump on her bed, when Robyn gave him a stern look.

Tyler began to tug on her hands. "C'mon."

"Go wash your face and brush your teeth. We have to get ready for church to celebrate Jesus' birthday, so open one gift for now."

Downstairs, Robyn watched her son survey the mass number of presents, more than she had planned at first. Two Scriptures came to mind: Genesis 50:20 and Job 42:12. The end result was better than what she had planned.

Finally, Tyler attacked the box wrapped in Transformers paper. She smirked. It was some type of boat from her mother. Ten minutes later, she coaxed her son upstairs for a bath.

"I want to wear my sweater!" he said as she pulled out his clothes, hoping Tyler would forget about the hideous holiday sweaters he'd picked out for himself and his father.

Derek rang the bell while she was setting the table. She answered the door to his smiling face and happiness shining from his eyes. Under his coat, the matching ugly sweater peeked through. He sniffed the air as she stepped back for him to enter with a bundle of gifts in his arms. The best gift he had given her besides his heart was her son. Not only physically, but allowing her to spend Christmas with Tyler despite the divorce decree that gave him child custody this holiday.

He brushed a kiss against her cheek. She would have been disappointed if he hadn't. "Merry Christmas, Mrs. Washington."

She let that slide, too. A month ago, she wouldn't have allowed him to share her space, much less use Mrs. "Merry Christmas."

Tyler hurried out of the kitchen, racing toward his father. "It's my birthday, Daddy! It's my birthday!"

"I know." They exchanged high fives. "Not only

is it your birthday, but it's Jesus', so we have to go to church and sing Happy Birthday to Him."

"Uh-huh," Tyler said distracted and reached for another the big box.

"Let's eat first," she told him as he rubbed his stomach.

Soon, all three were climbing in Derek's car for Holy Ghost Temple, their former church. Neither had attended regularly after their divorce, so Robyn didn't know what kind of reception they would receive with them walking in together—dismay or rejoicing.

Old and new members seemed glad to see them and commented on how handsome their son was. "Thank you," Derek answered for both of them. Surprisingly, Robyn's spirit settled in a comfortable place as if she'd never left.

Their former pastor, Elder Kinder, looked as if he hadn't aged a day when he stepped up to the podium after the choir's rendition of the "Hallelujah Chorus."

She silently whispered her thanks to God for the selection. It wasn't a coincidence.

"Merry Christmas, everyone." He lifted both arms to the congregation. "This is truly a Hallelujah day of praise."

"Mommy, he didn't say Happy Birthday to Jesus," Tyler whispered loudly, and others around them chuckled.

"I'm sure he will." Derek winked.

"Today, many of us have exchanged gifts with family and friends and it's not their birthday. I want you to think about it." He paused and folded his arms. She guessed he was waiting for them to do just that. "Please allow me to flip the script and talk about just a few of the gifts God has given us. The first was a wife, so Adam wouldn't go through life alone. Brothers, if you have one, take care of that gift."

Robyn could feel Derek's eyes on her, but she didn't want to focus on him at the moment.

The pastor continued, "From the first gift to the most expensive gift. It's a rather pricey sacrifice. King David said it best in 2 Samuel 24:24: *'Neither will I offer burnt offerings unto the LORD my God of that which doth cost me nothing.'* God wrapped Himself in the flesh and called Himself Jesus, according to the first chapter of John. Next, he took a beat down intended for us because of our sins—and there are many—and nailed them to the cross. He died, rose, and sent us the greatest gift we should celebrate every day: the Holy Ghost."

Robyn missed these in-depth, mind-stimulating sermons. She would rectify her absences by speaking with Elder Kinder after church. When he finished half an hour later, she looked at her ex-husband and couldn't find fault with him without examining herself.

As if knowing what she was thinking, Derek leaned over Tyler and whispered, "We survived a week as a couple. Can we extend our verbal agreement?"

"What do you have in mind?" More than anything, she wanted to re-establish her commitment to Christ. "Jesus has to be my priority."

"Mine too. I want us to start over with dating, dinner…"

She folded her arms in feigned defiance. "I want candy, flowers, and the works."

Winking, he bit his bottom lip while staring at hers. "You got it, Queen."

# CHAPTER TEN

Robyn blinked as she laid in her bed with a holiday hangover. She had overdosed on Derek Washington a day earlier, beginning with the Christmas service at church then celebrating Tyler's birthday at her house. It was definitely a family affair with Tyler's grandparents, uncles, cousins, and Erica and her hubby. It had been surreal really.

"Whew." She exhaled and smiled. Derek was stronger than indulging in a stiff drink, because his presence was drugging. Stretching, she involuntarily patted the other side of her bed. Of course it was empty. It had been two years since she shared her marriage bed with Derek.

Right after their divorce, it had been an adjustment. As the months turned to years, an empty bed became the norm. Why was she even thinking such thoughts? Maybe because their son was a mirror image of his daddy. Her heart fluttered at Derek's husky voice, hypnotic eyes and towering, imposing build.

Robyn rolled over, crossed her arms behind her head, and stared at the ceiling. She wasn't ready to get up and face the reality that she was indeed a divorcee with a mission of steering clear of her ex by any means possible. That was before the past few weeks' events.

What thoughts were on Derek's mind? she wondered. He was probably on his commute to work while she had taken the week off to be with Tyler, expecting to have a post-Christmas celebration because Derek had custody on even-year Christmases.

Because of Derek's generous offer, that didn't happen. Getting more comfortable under the covers, Robyn smiled, allowing her mind to recall the previous day's lasting memories. Whatever spot she found herself in the room, he was close by. All eyes seemed to be on them. She didn't have to lift a finger as he took charge of discarded gift wrappings and dirty dishes. After her guests left, he searched for her vacuum cleaner and went to work while advising Tyler how to help. "Rest," he instructed her with a twinkle in his eyes.

When was the last time she was pampered? She didn't argue and enjoyed the respite. Missing his closeness, she sought him out in the kitchen and slid next to him at the sink, but didn't say anything as he put plates back in the cabinet.

"I hope I've earned brownie points because I

haven't cleaned this much since my divorce." When she giggled, he returned her amusement with his own lopsided grin. "Hey, it's true."

Snatching a wet dish towel, she backed up, then popped him on the arm. His biceps seemed to ripple from her assault.

She had forgotten how much fun they used to have doing the simplest tasks. There was no doubt she still loved him, was attracted to him, or even wanted to kiss him, but they both had changed, and essentially didn't know the updated version of each other.

And that was her hesitation. Daydreaming was over. She had to get up and start her day before Tyler woke. The Christmas sermon had inspired her to reconcile her relationship with God first, then she could work on rebuilding one with Derek, so she got out of bed and slid to her knees.

"Thank You, Jesus for forgiving me and loving me…" After thanking him for her family and friends, she ended her morning prayer. Robyn quickly made her bed, then reached for her Bible. She had to get in the habit of feasting spiritually, then feeding her tummy.

As she read Philippians four, she backtracked to verse six: *Be anxious for nothing, but in everything by prayer and supplication let your requests be made known to God.*

The Lord knew she needed that message, because Derek made her nervous, and there was still the matter of the stability of her job. Should she jump ship amid speculations?

"Mommy, I'm hungry," Tyler said outside her door.

Standing, she crossed the room and opened the door. She smiled, noting the new Transformers pajamas he was wearing. "Before we eat, let's talk to Jesus." No time like the present to plant spiritual seeds in her son.

Confusion stretched across his face. "I talked to Him last night."

"Let's say good morning to Him."

"Hi, Jesus. Can I eat now?" He looked hopeful.

Robyn withheld a chuckle and rubbed his hair. "On your knees, buddy." She led him to the side of her bed and knelt with him, then guided him through a short prayer. Next, she headed to the kitchen, leaving him to make his bed and pick out his clothes. She smiled. It was refreshing to bring Christ back into her life.

Tyler wandered downstairs and made himself

comfortable at the table. "Is Daddy coming today?"

"He's at work, baby." Their marathon family time had ended at midnight. She didn't know what to expect from there on out. But she and Derek agreed to work on a possible reconciliation. Did divorcees date or pick a new wedding date?

"Can we go visit him?"

Definitely a daddy's boy and Derek's shadow. "I'll see if he has time to go to lunch with us."

"Can we go to McDonald's?"

"No." Her son had enough junk food on their outings last week, so she didn't have to think twice. During their breakfast of cream of wheat, fruit, and bacon, she listened to Tyler talk about his gifts and the dog he didn't get. Every time Tyler mentioned his Lego set, Derek's name came up.

"Can I have a baby brother to play with me since I can't have a dog?"

Robyn almost choked. When did a baby substitute for a pet? "Ah, ah…" Her heart pounded as she tried to come up with an answer. When the phone rang, Tyler scrambled out of his chair to answer it, then she exhaled.

The caller was no mystery by Tyler's animated tone. "We're going to lunch with you…"

Robyn shook her head and held out her hand for the phone. "Let me talk to your daddy."

"Okay." He gave it over, then hurried out of the room to play.

"Good morning, Mr. Washington, and I didn't say that."

"Mrs. Washington." He capped it with a husky chuckle. "I would love to see my most important people for lunch, but I have a conference call this afternoon."

She masked her disappointment as she pondered an excuse to see him. "If you want us to drop you off something to eat while we're out, we can." She tried to sound casual and nonchalant.

"I wouldn't mind seeing you."

His husky voice made her smile. "You will, later. You're coming for dinner three times this week, remember?"

"Who says I can't see you more than twice a day? I used to wake up to you and fall asleep—"

She cleared her throat and exhaled. Their G rated conversation was turning sensual. "We're no longer married, Derek. Those comments are inappropriate."

*Who says?* Derek wanted to ask his former wife— keyword: *former*—but he held his tongue. He couldn't push too fast. This time, he needed the Lord to order his steps. His mission was to remind her of the love they'd once shared in their marriage bed.

"Sorry. I'll behave. Your son's father is starving for a burger?" He snickered. The deli sandwich in the company refrigerator would keep another day, even if the expiration date was yesterday.

"You're so dramatic." She huffed, but Derek suspected it was fake. "We don't want to interrupt your work day, so what's a good time?"

"Before one-thirty." He paused. "As a matter of fact, you and Tyler can come now." *Back off, man,* he chided himself. Not only did that sound pushy, but desperate, which truth be told, he was.

"Umm-hmm. We'll see you between noon and one."

"And at six for dinner," he reminded her.

"Yeah. I'm feeding a man twice in one day, and he's not my husband."

Exactly. How long would they have to play house for their status to change? "Maybe, one day soon."

Robyn didn't take his bait with a comeback. Instead, she double-checked the company address since she had only visited once before they divorced.

"Thank You, Lord," he whispered when they ended the call. Grinning, he tackled his work with gusto, knowing that his family would be there soon.

Derek kept watching the time until finally he heard voices outside his closed office door, then his assistant buzzed him that he had guests in the lobby. Exhaling, he stood, checked his appearance and breath before opening the door and walking out.

"Dad!" Tyler's eyes widened as he raced his way. He lifted him in the air with one scoop as if he weighed ten pounds instead of forty-five.

"Hey, buddy." He immediately looked at Robyn who remained rooted in her spot in a chair. Next to her was a bag from Culver's Restaurant. His favorite place for hamburgers. He smiled, and she winked. He turned to his assistant. "Jasmine, this is my son."

She chuckled. "He said he was here to see his dad. One look and I knew who he belonged to."

"That's my boy, and this is Robyn."

"She's my mom," Tyler added.

The women exchanged nods before he ushered Tyler and Robyn inside his office. Since few of his colleagues had met Robyn, he toyed with how to introduce her: *ex-wife* and *former wife* sounded cold and the term *baby's momma* seemed cruel.

Situated in his seating area, Derek checked the time. He had exactly forty-seven minutes to enjoy their company. Tyler was a chatterbox while Robyn pulled out the restaurant's famous Butterburgers.

Tyler remained the center of attention as he said grace, then stuffed fries into his mouth.

"Yesterday was nice," he said before taking his first bite. He dabbed his mouth. "Thank you."

"Are you going to pay me for those sandwiches?" She chuckled as their son ate and bounced on the sofa.

"Tyler, stop," they said in unison.

"I planned to, but I was referring to us," he said softly. "Thank you for wanting to try."

She nodded, then cleared her throat. "What other major companies are in this building? I told you my job is unstable, and I want to start sending out my résumé."

*Woman, if we remarried, you wouldn't have to worry about another job.* He took another bite before answering. "Energizer is in the building next door." He named a few other companies to amuse her, but he was serious about her not stressing over income. "Robyn, if you let me, I'll make sure none of your bills are late."

After taking a sip from her cup, she shook her head. "I know you make good money and you've been more than generous with your monthly maintenance, but I don't expect you to take care of two households."

Exactly, which was reason enough for them to get back together soon. A knock on the door prevented him from replying. Craig Saunders, his IT manager, stuck his head in the door. "Hey, Derek, Kendall moved the meeting up—" He paused.

"Oh, I'm sorry. I didn't realize you weren't alone." He gave Robyn an appreciative assessment before locking his gaze on her legs.

"It's okay," she said, standing. "We were just leaving." She began to grab their trash.

That's it. His coworker rubbed him the wrong way. His actions were like a dog in heat, thinking that turning on his charm would get any woman he wanted. Not this time. What part didn't Craig understand that Robyn wasn't available? Craig seemed clueless as he reluctantly left, but Robyn seemed to pick up on his discomfort. "Jealousy is never a good asset."

Derek *hmph*ed. There was a difference between territorial and jealousy. As he was about to open the door, he overhead Craig and Jasmine talking.

"That man is a fool for letting a woman that fine get away. I know how to keep a woman happy."

"I wonder what happened," Jasmine said in a hushed voice. "The year I've been working for him, he's never mentioned his ex-wife. I assumed they didn't get along."

"His loss is another man's gain, but I think they're cordial for their kid's sake."

Derek crashed their private party with his appearance. He frowned at both of them. "I prefer to keep my private business private, so I hope this is the end of your conversation."

Clearly embarrassed, Jasmine nodded and took her seat behind her desk. Craig strolled down the hall toward the conference room as if he hadn't heard Derek's warning.

Fixing a smile on his face, he turned back to Robyn, who he hoped didn't hear anything, as she coaxed their son away from Derek's desk. He escorted them to the elevators where he hugged Tyler then Robyn. He hoped Craig was watching, because there would be no further silent warning.

# CHAPTER ELEVEN

After enjoying Derek at her dinner table twice and Bible class on Wednesday night, Robyn was disappointed when he called Thursday afternoon and canceled her invitation for dinner.

"I left work sick. I think I have the flu because I'm running a temperature. Sorry to bail on you and my boy tonight, but I don't want to get you two sick." He barked out a cough that seemed to drain him.

"You didn't get a flu shot?" Her ex never missed his doctor appointments and took all the necessary health precautions, which included flu shots every October.

"I can't remember. I've got to get some rest, babe. Talk to you later." He fumbled with his phone before disconnecting without her saying goodbye.

Minutes later, Tyler came out of his room into the kitchen. "What time is Daddy coming?"

"He's sick," she pouted, "so he's not coming."

Judging from the panic-stricken expression on her son's face, one would think Derek was in a coma, not suffering with a bout of the flu. Gnawing on his bottom lip, he looked at her. "Are you going to take care of him like you take care of me?"

"Well…" She hadn't planned on it. Derek was a big boy. She was sure he could doctor himself back to health. "Your grandma…"

Tyler shook his head. "No, I want you to take care of Daddy so he can get better."

It wasn't that she didn't care for Derek, or even love him, but under different circumstances, it wouldn't be a problem. Living in separate places had its benefits when dealing with infectious illnesses. She had to keep Tyler away so he wouldn't get sick. "If we pray for your father, Jesus will touch his body, okay?" she said, trying to comfort him.

"O-okay," he repeated, then yanked on her hand. "Hurry. I don't like my Daddy sick. He's supposed to play with me." On their knees, Tyler prayed until he sobbed. Robyn's heart broke for her child's love of his father.

A few hours later, Tyler was quiet as he ate his spaghetti and meatballs. Twice she had to remind him to take his elbows off the table. Robyn had lost some of her appetite too. When she hadn't heard from Derek after she put Tyler to bed, she phoned his mother.

"Hi, baby," Lane Washington greeted

cheerfully.

"Did you know Derek was sick?"

"No, I didn't. I guess that's why I haven't heard from him today."

"Tyler is beside himself. He wants me to go and be Derek's nurse." She chuckled at the uncertainty. "I told him his daddy is a big boy and I'm sure you'll make him some soup."

"Oh my. I had cataract surgery the day after Christmas. You know I wanted to wait until after the holidays so I could enjoy the family…"

Robyn had forgotten her mother-in-law had mentioned the surgery.

"I'm not supposed to—"

"No, don't concern yourself," Robyn said.

"My other sons don't know how to take care of a scratch. Plus, it's a fact my ex-husband's wife doesn't know how to cook…"

"No worries. I'll make Derek some soup and take it over," Robyn offered since she knew the request was coming.

Lane sounded relieved. "Bless you, honey. I know Derek is glad he has you."

"He doesn't have me anymore. We're working

on ourselves first."

"Umm-hmm." Lane asked about Tyler and thanked Robyn again for taking care of Derek. Robyn shook her head as they ended the call. This wasn't part of their reconciliation plan. Taking care of the sick wasn't on the dating and dinner list.

Tyler was ecstatic the next morning when he learned they were going to see Derek. "No, baby, you're going over Grandma Gibson's house and I'm going to check on your daddy. I can't take care of two sick people."

"But I can help you take care of Daddy," he whined with a pout.

Robyn wasn't budging on this one. "How about helping me make him some soup to feel better?"

Defiant, Tyler folded his arms.

"Little boy, if you don't change your attitude, then you'll be on punishment and when your daddy feels better you won't be able to play with him."

Tyler's expression changed real fast. "Sorry, Mommy. I want to help."

She called Derek, and he sounded worse. "I'm bringing you some soup."

"Okay." His voice faded before he ended the call.

Within an hour, Robyn was dicing baked chicken for soup. She never imagined taking care of her ex-husband during Christmas break. At least, she and Tyler had their flu shots, and she always made sure they had their daily dose of vitamin C. Was it was enough to keep her from getting sick?

To keep Tyler occupied, she had him color pictures for Derek until she finished cooking. Soon, she was ready to go and bundled up Tyler. After grabbing the containers, she set the alarm, then left. Once she dropped off Tyler, she thought about Derek. She knew where he lived for mailing purposes, but she'd never set foot in his place.

In hindsight, it seemed so petty for them to behave as complete strangers rather than cordial parents of an only child.

Taking care of him was the least she could do after tearing down the wall she had erected. She followed the GPS to 3769 Walnut Grove. It was a nice area with tree-line streets. She parked, gathered her items, and began the trek to the front door as gusts of wind ran circles around her legs. The temperature had definitely dropped. She buzzed the intercom to Apartment H and shivered.

"Robyn," Derek's hoarse voice greeted him.

"Yes." The door clicked, and she entered. She

eyed the doors until she came to Derek's. It was cracked. She pushed it open. "Hello," she yelled when she didn't see him.

"I'm back under the covers," he shouted from the bedroom.

She closed the door and scanned his place. The man had lived there two years and had very little furniture. A hotel room looked cozier. She wandered into the kitchen and began to unload her containers. She opened the fridge to find fruits, vegetables, and some leftover chicken. Shaking her head, she turned to the cabinets and began searching until she found a pot to reheat the soup.

Her heart pounded when she went in search of Derek's bedroom. Wasn't the bedroom off limits to a single woman? She had to remind herself that the man behind the closed door was once her husband and in need.

She knocked softly. "Derek," she said above a whisper, then pushed open the door. Meticulously decorated and furnished, it was neat except for the discarded tissues around the bed on the floor. "Derek?" He moaned and turned over. "You look horrible." She gasped.

"I feel it too. Thanks for coming, but I don't want to get you sick. Leave the food and go back home." He coughed and rolled over. His sorry state made her defiant.

"You're not the boss of me anymore, Mr. Washington." She moved closer and peered over the bed and chanced touching his forehead. He was burning up. "Have you taken any medicine?"

"Aspirin."

"That's not enough." She rummaged through his medicine cabinet. Aspirin was all there was. She needed to run to the store she'd passed on the way here, so she turned off the pot on the stove.

Back in the bedroom, she disturbed him again. "Derek—" she nudged him—"you need some real medicine and juices. Can I take your door key?"

He pointed to a drawer in the chest. "There's a spare key in the top drawer. It's yours."

She frowned. The only reason he got a spare key to her house was because of the break-in, and he promised not to use it unless no one had heard from them.

"Okay. I'll be right back."

"Take my credit card," he said in a hoarse voice until he succumbed to a coughing fit.

"I have money." She patted her purse. "Plus, my name isn't on it."

"Your name is Washington, and Washington is on the card. Just sign the receipt as Mrs. Washington."

She didn't argue and left. During the short trip, her mind was jumbled with conflicting emotions. Except for his bedroom, Derek's apartment resembled a man who had yet to unpack. The walls was bare and the furniture looked like it existed for necessity: sofa, two chairs, area rug and flat screen. The adjacent dining room consisted of a table for four. That's it.

Once she was inside Walgreens, she grabbed a cart and went shopping in record time, selecting everything she needed, and headed to the counter. Returning to the apartment, she lugged bags filled with soups, juices, brand name over the counter drugs, and plenty of disinfectant items. At his door, she fumbled with the key. First, she checked on her patient. She tipped in the room and returned his credit card in his wallet. He stirred.

"I spent almost sixty dollars, but you needed what I purchased. I hope that was okay."

His chuckle seemed forced. "You won't break my bank."

She smiled and backed out the room. There was a time when they argued that he accused her of doing that very thing—overspending. She wondered if he remembered that. Since he was resting, he could eat when he woke.

Strapping on a face mask and plastic gloves, she began to disinfect the apartment, opening windows despite the chill outside, to nurse Derek back to health.

The two-bedroom apartment was spacious, but too much square footage for a man who seemed to live in his bedroom. He definitely didn't entertain much. Why did that thought make her smile?

When she opened the other room where Tyler slept, she froze. It was as if she'd entered a different world. Her son's room was decorated with a colorful bedspread, matching window treatments, plush carpet and every gadget to delight any child. The walls' décor was a mixture of posters and pictures. This room felt like a home.

She wiped the doorknobs, then went quietly back into Derek's room and began to pick up behind him while cracking a window. That's when she noticed there was a dusting of snow. She should have checked the forecast.

In about an hour, she woke Derek. He opened his eyes and jumped.

"Woman, you scared me."

She giggled, forgetting about the mask. "Time to eat and take some real medicine. Afterward, she took a damp cloth and washed his face and neck and tucked him back into bed.

Her mother called right after he dozed off. "How's my son-in-law?"

Ex, she wanted to correct, but was in no mood to protest. "He's doing okay. He just needs some meds, food, and rest."

"And tender loving care." When Robyn didn't take the bait, her mother continued, "How long do you plan to stay over there?"

"Probably until his fever breaks. Then I'll have him take a shower while I change his sheets."

"Well, hopefully, that will be soon. We're supposed to get six inches of snow, so instead of going home, you and Tyler might want to spend the night here."

"Sounds good, Mom. I'll call you." Before she could push end, Tyler yelled in the background before getting on the line.

"Mommy, can I talk to Dad?"

"He's asleep, sweetie." After convincing the boy that she would have Derek call the moment he woke, her son seemed appeased. While Derek napped and with his apartment germ-free, she went back into Tyler's room and watched television.

She didn't realize she had dozed until the phone rang, and she jumped up to get it before it woke Derek. Her hand was on the receiver as the recorder kicked in. "Hi, Derek. This is Jasmine, calling to check in on you. I can't make it this evening, but I'll bring you some soup and goodies tomorrow to make you feel better."

Robyn lifted her brow and hmphed. Jasmine, Jasmine, she strained her mind to recall the face with the name and realized it was his assistant from work. How gracious that the pretty woman would prepare soup. But the "goodies" didn't sound like good intentions. If her ex already had a nursemaid, why was she there? Well, it appeared her services were no longer needed, because the only goodies she had was in the chicken and wild rice soup she'd made. The broth alone was good for his health.

In the middle of her mental fuming, the phone rang again. This time, she didn't try to get it, but waited to see if Jasmine would call back or whether it was another woman.

To her surprise it was their son. "Hi, Daddy. This is Tyler. Are you awake yet to talk to me? Mommy said you would call me and I don't know if she forgot to tell you. Okay. Bye, Daddy. Call me." The line went dead, and Robyn snickered.

That little boy was the best thing that came out of their marriage. Well, her duties there were done. She gathered her things and put up the fruit salad she'd made and was about to advise Derek she was leaving when her mother called again. ""Baby, I think you may need to stay where you are tonight."

*Uh-uh.* She was out of there. "My keys are in my hand. He's sleeping, and I should be there in about twenty minutes."

"Look outside. The snow is coming down heavy. "I don't think you should chance it. Tyler is fine, and if you get stranded, that will only make us worry, and probably Derek too."

Robyn raced to the window, and indeed the street was covered and so was her car. *Great.* "Mom, I don't think that's a good idea…"

"Stay and take care of your husband."

"Ex," she said as her mother ended the call. Gritting her teeth, Robyn was beyond upset. Not only had she not planned to spend the night, but apparently Derek had other interests.

"Robyn? Robyn, are you still here?" Derek's faint voice came from his bedroom.

She had a mind not to answer, but in her heart she knew Derek still loved her. When he was sleeping, Robyn had used the quiet time to silently pray about how to proceed with their relationship.

"Who was on the phone?"

Leaning against the doorjamb, she crossed her arms. She had her coat on and keys jingling from her hand. "Your son…"

"Our son." He smiled. Tyler meant the world to him— both of them. "And?"

"Jasmine. She's bringing over soup and goodies tomorrow."

He frowned at Robyn's lifted brow. "Why would she do that?"

"I was hoping you knew why, because if there is some interest there—"

"My only interest is my family—you and Tyler. Plus, she's married." Derek cut her off. His body might be weak, but his mind was on high alert. "I don't think her husband will be riding shotgun. "She's my assistant and nothing more." He covered a yawn then scratched the hairs on his chin. "You leaving?"

"I planned on it, but it's snowing."

"I don't want you driving in—" Derek backtracked. He had no say in her decisions. "You're welcome to stay—overnight. Although, I'm sorry I'm not a better host." He yawned again and smacked his lips. "Do you have any more soup and cornbread?"

"Sure." She turned to do his bidding, but he stopped her. "Babe, God is my witness. The only woman I want is five-feet-six inches tall and has beautiful brown eyes to match her golden brown hair. Trust was never an issue between us, so I hope you believe me."

She glanced over her shoulder. "I do."

Derek exhaled as he watched her disappear. He could only think of hearing those words off her lips at the altar when she became his wife again, this time forever.

Feeling a tad better, Derek lay on his back and stared at the ceiling. How could he not have gotten his yearly flu immunization? He remembered he had taken a business trip and had missed the day the company sponsored the free shots.

It would take mental, physical, and spiritual strength and endurance to win Robyn back. He sighed and rubbed his face. He must look like a mess, but at the moment, his options were few. He was too weak to shower and shave. Minutes later, he could smell the brew before she opened his door and carried the bowl on a tray. He scooted up in bed and covered his mid-section. She situated the tray on his lap, then felt his forehead. "You're still a little warm. I think you need some more medicine and rest."

"Okay, but I've got to call my boy back."

"What about Jasmine?"

"Jasmine is my assistant. I don't owe her a call back."

She nodded, then handed him the cordless phone. "Good answer."

"Hey, buddy," he said after his mother-in-law put Tyler on the phone.

"I thought you forgot."

Derek ate and listened as Tyler told him about the snow and his grandma helping him make a baby snowman. Robyn returned and took his empty bowl. He winked.

When she came back with a glass of juice and medicine, he hurried off the phone. "I have to take a nap now."

"I take naps too. Mommy says…." Robyn must have sensed their son was on another talking binge when she took the phone.

"Daddy will talk to you later. Bye, sweetie." Then she turned to him with a warm smile and a cool towel, which she applied to his face and neck. "Now, take this." She handed over the glass and pills.

"I appreciate you," he said softly as he accepted her offering.

"I know." She cleared her throat. "Ah, I didn't prepare to spend the night. Do you have a T-shirt I can wear?"

He pointed to the top dresser drawer. As he watched her, Derek tried to keep his mind off the things a man desired in the bedroom.

# CHAPTER TWELVE

"I didn't sign up for this," Robyn mumbled as she tidied Derek's kitchen. Who would have thought a month ago, or even three weeks earlier, she and her ex would be on speaking terms? The real shocker was she was spending the night at his apartment, a place she'd vowed not to step foot inside.

His place lacked the warmth of a home, no pictures or personal touches to say welcome. How could he stand it? The only exception was the bedrooms where there was more than one piece of furniture, colors to hint at the owners' personality, and just enough of messy to indicate someone lived there.

Behind the closed doors of her son's room, Robyn changed into Derek's T-shirt. As she wiggled it over her head, she recalled the times that his undershirts were her pajamas of choice. Now, it felt odd. There was such a big gap missing out of their lives, and she wondered if it would close—as the saying goes, time heals wounds. She believed that to an extent, but what about when they quarreled, would they bring up the past?

She cleared her head before kneeling to say her

prayers, "Jesus, did You set me up? I know in Your sight Derek and I are probably still husband and wife, but we're divorced according to man's law. All I ask is that Derek and I find our way back to each other because of our love and not our son." After giving thanks for all things and sending up petitions on behalf of others, she said Amen.

As soon as her head rested on the pillow, she drifted to sleep.

Robyn jerked as she rolled over and teetered on the edge to keep from tumbling off the juvenile size bed. Once she steadied herself, she opened her eyes. She blinked until her surroundings came into focus. Reaching for her phone, she noted that it was three in the morning. Despite the uncomfortable bed, she was surprised she had gotten some sleep.

Getting up, she decided to check on Derek. She heard his light snore as she opened his door and quietly approached his bed. He didn't move as she touched his forehead. He was still a bit warm, but not burning up. She pulled the covers up to his chin, and whispered a soft prayer, "Jesus, You are the restorer of health. I ask that You breathe into his body and strengthen his bones, in Jesus' name. Amen." She used the bathroom and climbed back in her temporary bed.

The next morning, the day before the new year, Robyn was back in Derek's kitchen, preparing breakfast for her patient when Erica called to check in.

"You're a naughty girl spending the night at a man's house," her friend teased. "Oooh. I'm going to tell." She giggled, then added, "Excellent!"

"Derek was sick. I brought him some soup and got snowed in," Robyn explained.

"Sounds like a perfect plot of a romance novel to me. So how is my friend doing?" Her playful tone turned serious.

"Hopefully his fever broke overnight, and I'm about to go check on him, so bye." She grabbed a bowl and scooped up a serving of oatmeal, adding a tad of butter and cinnamon. She placed it on a plate and arranged toast and orange slices around it.

Derek was awake when she entered his room. "Hey. How you feeling?"

"Better that you're still here." He mustered a smile. "Your tender loving care brought me back from the brink of death."

Drama. She *tsk*ed. "You were running a temperature not lying in a coma." She steadied the food tray on his lap as he scooted up. "You'll get my bill. Here's breakfast. Eat to regain your strength."

"Robyn, you still look pretty in the morning."

"And you look horrible," she half-joked.

"Seriously, nothing about you has changed, not a wrinkle or gray strand," he continued to flatter her.

Nothing took away from Derek's handsomeness—not even sick, pale, and bad breath. "I have changed."

"I guess we both have. But I was talking about your beauty." He looked down at the tray and frowned. "Hey, I thought I smelled bacon and eggs."

"You did. That's my breakfast. This is yours. Bon appétit." Laughing, she walked out the room despite his protests. She had real food on the kitchen table waiting for her.

She had barely finished her meal when her mother called. "How's Derek?"

"He looks better this morning. I just gave him breakfast."

"Well, your son wants to see him."

She chuckled. "I'm sure he does, considering he hasn't seen both of us in a day, but I haven't taken Derek's temperature."

"He can wear a mask. I'm sure you bought more

than one," Derek's deep voice drew her attention as he stood in the doorway. "It's New Year's Eve, and I would like all of us to be together. We had planned to go to Watch Meeting, remember?"

She did her best to keep her eyes focused on his face and not his bare chest. Where was the T-shirt he had on earlier? She forced her mind back to her phone conversation. "Ahh, maybe I can bring him later. I really want to go home and freshen up."

"No need, I'll bring you a change of clothes from your stash here, and I'll bring my grandson to his father, so no need to leave. See you in a few hours." *Click.*

Frustrated that everyone, including God, seemed to be giving her an overdose of Derek Washington. She needed baby steps, not twenty-four-hour shifts. She really craved some space.

*Let patience have her perfect work,* God whispered, calming her spirit.

Taking a deep breath, she fixed a smile and turned back to Derek. "I see you're up. I'm glad you feel better."

"Thanks to God answering your prayer. I heard you whispering last night and thought I was dreaming. When I opened my eyes you were gone, but your fragrance lingered."

She blushed, then changed the subject. "You're about to have company—our son. You're still weak, so it won't take long for Tyler to zap whatever energy you've regained. Since you're up, feel like taking a shower and putting on some fresh clothes while I disinfect your bedroom?"

While Derek showered, Robyn went to work changing the linens, spraying the bed, and opening the windows to air out the room. Once her mother got there with her clothes, she would shower too. It hadn't been twenty minutes later when Robyn put clean sheets on the mattress when Derek's doorbell rang. Her mother was early.

Hurrying to the door, she expected to see her son. Instead, she blinked at the sight of Jasmine. Judging from what she had on, the woman was wearing her goodies.

"Jasmine, what are you doing here?" Derek asked, coming out the bathroom, wearing a pair of sweats and a T-shirt. His attire was modest compared to what his assistant was wearing, provocative to say the least. She boasted her curves in leggings and a mid-thigh over-sized white turtle-neck sweater, standing in heels that seemed like a mile high. What in the world was going on? She remained in the hallway with a surprised expression on her face that was overkill in makeup. He had never seen this seductive side of his conservative assistant.

It didn't look like Robyn was about to invite her in. How did she even get inside his building without being buzzed in? Probably a neighbor. He padded across the floor and opened the door wider.

"I called. Didn't you get my message?" Inviting herself in, Jasmine stepped around him.

"As a matter of fact, I gave him your message," Robyn said with an edge to her voice.

Uh-oh. Derek had never been in the crossfire of two women, so he was clueless of what was about to go down. *Jesus, I'm too weak to deal with this. Help.*

"What did you cook?" Robyn asked casually as she bumped Derek out of the way and closed the door.

*Really?* Derek eyed his former wife with suspicion. *Should I be relieved that's all she has to say?*

"P–Pot roast," Jasmine stuttered, suddenly appearing uncomfortable, either by Robyn's presence or maybe the getup she was wearing.

"Ah," Derek didn't know what to say.

"Go home to your husband, honey" Robyn said

sweetly. "I'm sure he'll enjoy it—and hurry. I heard the temperature is going to drop and the wind will cut right through your leggings."

Embarrassed, the woman spun around, opened the door and came face to face with Derek's mother, mother-in-law, and Tyler as they barged into the apartment. She hurried out without looking back. Judging from their curious expressions, Derek had some explaining to do. He mustered a smile, wondering what had happened to the building security. Was the entrance suddenly a free-for-all?

Before Tyler could have full reign, Robyn removed his coat, then fitted a mask over his nose and mouth. He thought it was cool.

His own mother kept her distance as she headed to his kitchen, carrying a pot. "Hey, son. How are you feeling? I made you some pot roast."

He exchanged a glance with Robyn who started laughing uncontrollably. "Our favorite."

Mrs. Washington asked, "Who was that chile who left here half-naked?"

"A desperate housewife," Robyn answered before he could, then shoved a mask in his chest to put on around Tyler.

"Married?" Mrs. Washington blinked.

"I guess she forgot to remove her wedding ring." Robyn smirked and walked ahead of him into the kitchen with a little sway in her hips that made him smile.

# CHAPTER THIRTEEN

Robyn squinted at her mother who went beyond the call of duty to bring her a change of clothing. Since when did she own a wine-colored sweater and wear it with the price tag still attached? And the fashionable jeans were labeled as form-fitting. "Really?"

Sara shrugged. "The ones at my house were too blah, so I stopped by Marshalls and purchased a new one and couldn't resist the sale on the pants, then I saw matching earrings and an on-sale emergency makeup compact."

"There is no emergency." Robyn sighed.

"Yeah, you keep thinking that. That woman who showed up is proof that other women want what God gave to you." She emphasized her words with a nod.

"Mom, that woman is married."

"That woman was in heat. *Hmph*ed." She grunted. "Now get busy while I visit with my son-in-law."

*No man was worth fighting for,* she thought as she rumbled through the bag on the path to the shower. Especially a man who divorced her—no, she divorced him.

*A good husband and marriage is worth defeating the devil*, God whispered.

Could she and Derek reconcile and be a happily married couple again as if the years apart hadn't happened? Her biggest fear was being taken for granted because they shared a son. She meant what she'd told Derek: She wanted the courtship, flowers, and the whole romance package—he needed to woo her as if it was the first time they'd met.

Jasmine said she was bringing the goodies. Robyn laughed, scrutinizing the items in her sack, Sara Gibson had brought the treats. Her mother had thrown in a scented bath gel and lotion. She showered, then dressed in the new top and jeans. After hooking the earrings on, she opened the emergency makeup face repair kit and dabbed her cheeks with blush, stroked mascara on her lashes, and rounded off her look with lip gloss.

She wasn't glamorous, but it was enough in case another Jasmine wanted to drop off a home-cooked meal to Derek.

Refreshed, she stepped out of the bathroom to find her mother and mother-in-law were gone. They hadn't stay long. Wearing matching white masks, Tyler jumped up while Derek's eyes sparkled.

"You look pretty," Tyler said.

"Yeah, Mommy," Derek added.

"Thanks." She wiggled her toes. At least she'd a recent pedicure. "Do you have a pair of socks I could use?"

"You can scavenger hunt through my drawers to find a match."

She chuckled. "Some things never change."

Minutes later, they lunched on pot roast, then played one of Tyler's games. When she noticed Derek was fighting to keep his eyes open, she announced nap time for both the Washington men.

While they slept, she glanced out the window at the streets that were somewhat passable. How had her mother braved the weather with a small child in tow, then had the nerve to go shopping? The day was dreary, so Robyn claimed a spot on the sofa and took her a nap. What a way to spend New Year's Eve.

Before long, she heated the TV dinners she had purchased at Walgreens. Afterward, the threesome watched a movie in Derek's bedroom. It was a good thing she had her son wearing a mask, because he was clinging to his father as if Derek was going to vanish.

"I really wanted to go to church and start the year off right with my family and God," Derek mumbled while Tyler was engrossed in a dinosaur movie.

"Surprisingly, we're still speaking, Tyler's happy, and God is in our midst. I say that is a great combination to bring in the new year.

Derek couldn't remember the last time he had watched so much television. One movie seemed to fade into another one. Robyn sat in the chair next to his bed while Tyler was huddled under his arm. Since Holy Ghost Temple had a live stream, they decided to watch it. He didn't object when she sat on the bed next to him when the church service started.

As they listened to the saints testify about God's goodness throughout the year, Derek only had to reflect on the past weeks when his life changed. The choir sung two songs, then their pastor stood at the podium.

"It's almost midnight," he began. "I'm not talking about our watches, but God's timing. Are you ready for Jesus' return? Playtime is over. In the twenty-fifth chapter of Matthew, there were ten virgins who were slack about the groom's return. Are you? They were invited to the feast, but didn't fill their lamps with oil. The oil represents the Holy

Ghost. Whatever is broken in your life, why not take it to Jesus, so He can fix it and fill you with His spirit? Pastor paused and rubbed his chin. "Let me come in a different way. How many of you have moved from one place to another?"

Derek saw hands raise. He glanced at Robyn, but she was focused on the screen.

Elder Kinder shrugged as he scanned the audience. "I'm always bewildered by folks who move junk from their old residence to the new one. A new house means it's new, fresh, clean—like the Holy Ghost. Don't take old stuff to your new house and into your new year…"

Derek squeezed Robyn's hand. She looked at him. "As I move forward into the new year, I thank the Lord that you're with me."

Her eyes watered. "Me too."

He kissed her forehead, then Tyler's, who remained knocked out, then turned his attention to the sermon. At midnight, the church celebrated with praise. "Happy New Year…" He faced Robyn, only to see she had drifted off to sleep. He watched her even breathing. She had to be tired, taking care of him and his needs with little complaining.

She and Tyler had him wedged in, so he shifted slowly until he was free from their entrapment. He quietly lifted his son and carried him to his room. After washing Tyler up and changing him into pajamas, Derek slipped him under the covers. Finally, he got on his knees and thanked God for his precious son.

When he returned to his room, he smirked at Robyn who was balled up. He pulled the covers over her. Stepping back, Derek stared before brushing his lips against her forehead. One day soon—real soon, he hoped to be married again to her. Yawning, he made a bed for himself on the sofa. Yep, this time next year, he would be a married man.

Robyn snuggled under the covers and smiled. She was about to roll over, but something behind her wouldn't move. Her eyes flew open. Oh no. She was still at Derek's, in his bed and evidently, lying next to him. She turned to give him a piece of her mind and realized it was Tyler. Exhaling, she rubbed her son's head as he quietly watched her. "Where's your daddy?"

He pointed toward the cracked door. "On the couch asleep. I want to go to my house, Mommy."

"Me too. Let's check on your dad first." Last evening, he seemed to have regained his strength.

She got up and peeked out into the living room. Derek's body was half on the sofa and half on the floor. Crossing her arms, she chuckled at the sight. Still on the mend, the man needed his rest in a comfortable bed, yet he had given up his for her. That was love. Tyler was about to cross the room to Derek when she stopped him, putting a finger to her lips. *Shh.*

She guided him back into the bedroom and grabbed a pillow and encouraged her son to do the same. Grinning, they tip-toed across the hardwood floor. Standing over her ex, she stared at his profile to confirm her earlier assessment. He definitely looked much better. Even with the shadow of a beard across his jaw, he was a fine specimen of a man. She gave Tyler a silent count: one, two three… She lifted her pillow and began her assault. Giggling, Tyler followed suit. Derek snatched their son's pillow with one hand.

"One down, one to go." He growled, mimicking an animal.

"I don't think so." Robyn held on to her weapon for dear life.

Before her eyes, he lifted her off her feet into the air, then dumped her on the sofa and began to tickle her.

"Stop, stop," she screamed and laughed, then just as suddenly, he pulled back. "I'm glad you feel better."

"Yep. I had this fantastic nurse. How about I cook my favorite people breakfast?"

"After we all freshen up." She giggled and raced to his bathroom to be the first to brush her teeth. Who knows? They might share their first kiss of the year.

# CHAPTER FOURTEEN

It was bittersweet for Robyn when she, Tyler, and Derek had said their goodbyes the day before. He had accompanied her and Tyler home, stayed a few hours, and returned to his boring apartment—her description—to get rest for the new work week. They decided to eat dinner together as a family as much as possible. Although he had offered to cook dinner twice a week, Robyn thought it would be more nutritious for her to prepare the meals.

She strolled into her office seconds after her boss signed for a floral delivery. He glanced up at her with a smirk. "For you. I guess you had a good Christmas."

Robyn blushed. "One that I could never have imagined."

"Well, get settled in, then we'll chat," Mr. Rolland said and walked down the hall to his office. The man had been her employer for ten-plus years. He had witnessed her happiness at being a wife and mother and sadness at becoming a divorcée and single mom. Clearly, he wanted the scoop behind her smile.

She quickly unlocked her desk and stored her

things in the drawer before ripping off the wrapping from her delivery. She never could get too many flowers, or run out of a spot to display them. As Derek probably suspected, the colorful arrangement drew her in. she took a whiff, then read the small card.

*Thank you for giving me a Merry Christmas and a Happy New Year. Call me when you get a chance.*

*Love,*

*D*

Before she got busy, she texted him. The flowers are beautiful.

Seconds later, he called instead of replying. "Beauty is in the eye of the beholder, and my vision becomes clearer every time I see you."

His husky voice and sweet words made Robyn's heart flutter. Her response choked in her throat. It was surprising how Derek could make her happy just being himself. "Thank you."

"How about lunch?"

She picked up a pen and tapped it on her desk. "I would like that, but I don't think I want to come back to your office between Carnal Craig and Jezebel Jasmine." She chided herself for her descriptive terms, then felt bad. "Sorry. I shouldn't have said that."

"You are free to come and visit any time. Jasmine is walking on eggshells after that unprofessional stunt of showing up at my place uninvited. My intention was to fire her this morning for improper conduct, but I heard God tell me no, so I gave her a stern warning instead. The last thing I need is office gossip about an affair with a married woman." He paused. "Correction: I guess I am having an affair with a woman who I was once married to."

"That's not funny. If I was a jealous woman and insecure, you and I might not be on speaking terms."

"But you know who has my heart," he said in a husky, low voice.

"Yes, I do, and I miss you, so be here by noon."

"I miss you more. See you soon, babe."

Robyn exhaled. What a way to begin a morning: flowers and being in love again.

Disconnecting, Derek smiled. He had four hours and counting. He thought about his assistant. Jasmine could thank the Lord for keeping her job.

He never knew the woman had any romantic attractions toward him. As soon as she had arrived at work a few hours earlier, God had given him the words to say. Derek had opened his office door and stepped out. She jumped and looked like a squirrel caught stealing a nut. "Jasmine, thanks for your concern during my illness, but under no circumstances are you to visit my home uninvited. Our relationship is strictly business."

The horror on her face was amusing, but Derek wasn't laughing. He might have messed up his marriage, but he had no intentions of messing up someone else's.

As long as he had been her boss, he never suspected that she and her husband were having problems. But it wasn't his place to advise her to work on it by any means necessary, or she may regret it later.

"I apologize, and I did as your ex-wife suggested and took the pot roast home to Gary. He enjoyed it." She offered a faint smile as she twisted her fingers.

"Glad to hear it, and for the record, I'm committed to one woman, and that ex-wife will soon be my wife again, so she will be visiting here often. I assume you will show her the utmost respect."

"Yes, sir. No problem." Jasmine swallowed and seemed to be glad when her phone rang so she had an excuse to end their discussion.

Then there was the matter of Craig. The man didn't take hints. Derek spied Craig coming from the restroom. "Just the man I want to see."

"What's up, man? Welcome back. Glad to see you've recovered."

Derek slipped his hands in his pockets. Robyn said she wasn't a jealous woman. He couldn't claim that victory where she was his concern. "Robyn took excellent care of me."

Craig snickered. "Man, if I had an ex-wife like her, she wouldn't be my ex."

"Exactly." He nodded. "Which is why she won't be much longer. We're working on reconciling our marriage, so she's not available for your roaming eyes. You're still on probation. You could be the first one in years to receive an unflattering review in your file."

An unreadable expression draped his face until he responded, seemingly reluctantly. "Understood."

With those mindless tasks taken care of, he strolled back to his office, thanked God for restraint, and began his day until it was time to see Robyn.

Hours later, driving the thirty minutes across town to take Robyn to lunch was worth the distance. Although they loved Tyler, they needed some alone time, and he craved those private moments. He parked and trekked toward the building entrance in anticipation of seeing Robyn.

He hadn't been to her job in so long, he had to scan the directory to locate the company. As soon as he entered her office, Derek felt something was wrong. The sparkle in her eyes was gone as she finished a call. Then she stood and mustered a smile that appeared too heavy for her lips to pull off. "What's wrong?" He repeated the question when she didn't answer.

"I'll tell you," she whispered as he guided her arms into the sleeves of her coat.

Taking her hand, he led her outside to the parking lot. She said nothing. Once they were in his car, he started the ignition and faced her. "Talk to me."

Her tears came before her words. "It's official. Mr. Randall is closing the business before the year is out." Dazed, her lips trembled. Robyn blinked, but it still seemed as if she was staring right through him. She rambled on, "He knows people will start jumping ship, so he's offering a large severance pay and bonus for those who stay until the end." He gathered her in his arms and pulled her closer. "What am I going to do? I've always worked, except for the months I stayed at home with our son."

That problem solved. It was a no-brainer to take care of her needs as a husband was expected to do. She didn't have to work. Derek made sure he was frugal with his expenses so that she and Tyler would lack nothing. He had it all figured out when he brought her hand to his lips.

*This is not about you. Listen to what she wants,* his mind coaxed him, so he asked instead, "Want me to pray with you?"

She faced him. "Yes."

Closing his eyes, he petitioned God. "Lord, in the name of Jesus, I wish I could be her hero on this, but I can't. We need You to show us Your will concerning her next move. Comfort her and give her peace, and please give me the strength to take care of her. In Jesus' name. Amen."

"Amen." She sniffed and exhaled. Robyn sat quiet then looked at him. "Now that that's out the way, I think I'm ready to eat."

# CHAPTER FIFTEEN

Derek had changed. He surprised Robyn by supporting her decision to begin her job search. She had expected him to go macho on her and call the shots, suggesting she stay at home. Being gainfully employed was about her self-worth as a professional woman. Unfortunately, it had been a couple of weeks, and not one response from the dozen of résumés she had sent.

Erica called after she had fed Tyler breakfast Saturday morning. "Have anything planned this weekend?"

"Nope. I plan to stay in all weekend, except for church tomorrow."

"Girl, you need to get out," her friend pleaded. "My treat. It's Derek's weekend with Tyler, right?"

Robyn sat on a counter stool in the kitchen and looked out the window. "Actually, we did away with his or her weekends. He's coming over later, and we plan to stay in and make sandwiches for lunch, order pizza for dinner and watch dinosaur movies until Tyler goes to sleep."

"Hmm. Well, dare I interfere with the love birds." Erica paused. "I'm sorry about your job situation, but I'm so glad Derek is by your side. I'm praying for my favorite people."

"I just don't want to feel desperate for a man and job. I don't want my circumstances to cloud my judgment," she said in a low voice, glancing over her shoulder for signs of Tyler popping up nearby.

"Everything is going to work out according to God's plan. Just don't block your blessing this time."

They chatted for a few more minutes until Derek's signature ring alerted her of his arrival. Funny that was one thing she couldn't get enough of this time: Derek Washington's presence.

The weeks rolled into February, and Robyn had one phone interview out of twenty applications. She discussed with Derek whether to stay on until the company closed.

"I think that's a wise choice. Whatever you need, just ask me," he had said unselfishly.

She smiled, believing him.

Days later on Valentine's Day, flowers were delivered at her house before she walked out the front door. At her office, a larger bouquet was waiting for her. She was as giddy as a high school teenager.

Before she could get settled, a fruit assortment

arrived at her desk. This time, a note from her baby: To my sweetest Mommy. Love, Tyler.

She smiled and sniffed. She had a lot to be thankful for. She called Derek. "Hi."

"Hi back. How is my sweetheart this morning?"

"I'm happy."

"And I love you. My heart never stopped. Thank you for being my valentine. See you at five-thirty. Have a blessed day, baby."

To hear Derek say those words made her heart flutter. Her words choked in her throat until the only things she could say was, "You too."

Although she was leaving early, the time seemed to crawl. Finally, she left for her hair appointment.

At home, the time sped by as she tried to get ready. Although red was so cliché for Valentine's Day, it was her best color, so she donned it anyway.

Her doorbell rang at five-thirty. She opened the door to see Derek standing on the porch. The glow from her overhead porch light seemed to illuminate his features, especially the sparkle in his eyes. A black limo waited at the curb.

"Ms. Washington."

"Mr. Washington." He stepped forward and handed her a single rose. She took a whiff then chuckled. "More flowers."

He nodded. "You have my heart, Robyn, and as you carry this flower, you are carrying my heart in your hands, so handle with care—now don't crush the petals."

Twirling it between her fingers, she realized it was void of thorns to pierce her own heart. "I won't." They stared into each other's eyes until Derek stepped in and backed her into the foyer where he helped her with her wrap.

On their ride from North St. Louis County to downtown Clayton, Robyn snuggled against his chest and closed her eyes. This was the most celebrated romantic evening of the year where every single lady wished for a proposal. Unlike so many other women who waited for that special moment, imagining a lifetime together, Robyn had lived the good times and bad times with the man who had her wrapped in his arms. With their renewed spiritual walk with the Lord Jesus, Robyn was ready to taste that happiness again.

"What are you thinking about?" he whispered in her ear.

Smiling, she shook her head. "Private thoughts."

Their driver double parked on Wydown in front of Bar Les Freres, a French restaurant known for its pricey menu. When they walked inside, she noticed the intimate settings for two were uniformed throughout. The red brick walls and eye-catching chandeliers pulled her into the romantic ambiance. They were shown to their table. Derek kissed her neck as he assisted in removing her coat. "How's my heart—I mean flower—holding up?"

"It's protected."

The waitress appeared and welcomed them, then advised them of the Valentine's menu specials. Both chose the fillet mignon. Once they were alone, Derek reached across the table and squeezed her hands. "For the past few months, I've learned so much about you, my son's beautiful mother. You've changed—"

She stopped him. "I've matured as a person."

"I have too," he admitted. Their salads arrived when he was about to say more, instead he gave thanks and asked God to bless their meal.

As Robyn nibbled, her heart pounded, waiting for the perfect moment, the perfect question coming from the perfect man for her.

It was time, Derek thought as he fingered the ring box in his pants pocket. It appeared a couple of other guys had beaten him to his knee in popping the question. After removing the napkin from his lap, he stood, then knelt. Robyn's skin seemed to glow as she looked at him expectantly.

He took a deep breath to extract every emotion from his heart. "When I asked you to be my wife eight years ago, I promised you the world." He choked back all the past regrets and disappointments he had caused her. "But I failed as a man, not depending on God to show me how to love my wife. Although we've changed, God never changes, neither does His Word. Second chances aren't to be taken for granted—in love and with God." He massaged her fingers when her hands began to tremble. "Yet, I've found favor with Jesus to be blessed with both."

She acknowledged his truth with a tender smile.

"Thieves not only robbed you of your wedding ring, but the devil stole our happiness. Tonight, at this very moment, I'm here to claim what the devil kidnapped from me—and you." He paused to lift the token from its box. "This new diamond represents the new man God has molded for you. Although this is the second time I'm asking you to trust me with your heart, I'm confident that whatever years were taken from us, God will multiply our latter years to be greater like he did Job. Please mend my broken heart and marry me, Ms. Washington."

"Yes," she whispered as faint claps floated around them.

He slipped the ring on her finger and pulled her from her chair for a lingering, promising kiss.

Her lids fluttered as he pulled away. Robyn swallowed. "This will make one little boy and our mothers happy." She smiled.

"Yes, it will, considering our son helped me pick out the ring, and even wrote down what I should say." They both laughed, but Robyn shook her head.

"I can't believe he didn't blabber the secret."

"It's a man thing." He winked. "Seriously, I told him I didn't need any help in that department." He reached inside his jacket pocket, and pulled out his cell phone, then tapped a number and Tyler's voice came on the speaker. "Mommy said yes."

He screamed his excitement and they chuckled. Robyn could hear her mother in the background, praising the Lord.

"See, Dad, I told you to marry my mommy," he began to ramble until Derek cut him short. They both told Tyler they loved him before ending the call.

Robyn exhaled once they were seated again, she stared at the ring, wiggling her fingers. "This is so bittersweet. I had planned to celebrate three years as a divorcée on a tropical island."

*My Word is sweet to the lips, but My judgment for those disobeying Me is bitter,* God whispered. *Read Ezekiel 3 and Revelation 10 and see if I will not perform the works I set out to do. Your love will be a witness of My love to those who have divorced Me from their lives.*

Derek wasn't quite sure what Jesus had in store for them. He was hopeful they would make it this time by keeping God as the center for a testimony that marriages between a man and woman work. "Let's void out that dark celebration with a joyous one by getting remarried on the anniversary of our divorce, then taking that trip," he paused, getting caught up in the moment. "I mean, if that's okay with you, babe."

She placed her hands on both sides of his jaw and drew him closer. "You lead, and I'll follow. Maybe the judge who presided over our divorce will remarry us."

Grinning, Derek liked the idea. What better way to override their divorce than by the judge who granted it. "I'll call tomorrow and find out." He crossed his fingers, then texted the limo driver that they were ready.

After Robyn gathered her purse and coat, Derek escorted her to the entrance amid a few congratulations. Almost in unison, they thanked the well-wishers.

While waiting in the lobby, a couple approached them. They appeared older—or seasoned as his mother would correct him. "Excuse me. My name is James Webster, and this is Cynthia," he seemed to struggle to add, my wife. "We're getting a divorce, but I couldn't help but overhear your proposal—or re-proposal. After thirty-seven years of marriage, this week we decided to make this our parting dinner on Valentine's Day."

Derek's heart twisted. He and Robyn barely made it to six years before calling it quits. He exchanged a glance with his second time around fiancée and wondered what was she thinking? "I'm sorry to hear that."

James played with the brim of his hat. "Listening to your sincere words made me think about regrets." He stared at his wife, then reached for her hand. "Our love was once strong."

"We want that back, but too many hurts have gotten in the way over the years. Staying together any longer would only make us miserable," the petite woman spoke up. She was nice-looking in her mature years, but Derek guessed she was probably stunning in her youth. "You two are making us question if we wasted our lives together. What turned it around for you?" Her eyes were wide with a mixture of hope and curiosity.

"We thought it was our little boy. He simply wanted his mommy and daddy to be a family, and the Lord let us know what he had given us was a gift," Derek said as he drew Robyn closer. "Marriages don't have to fail if husbands and wives have God on their side."

"We chose to walk away from our blessing," Robyn added, "but the devil is a liar. God can restore your marriage, but you're going to have to let Him restore your heart, mind, and soul. Do you mind if we pray for you?" They shook their heads.

Derek nodded and urged him into a corner for privacy. The four held hands and Derek prayed softly, "Jesus, James and Cynthia need You." He paused as grappled for the right words to say.

*Speak what I speak to you,* God whispered. "If you return to Me, and repent, I can heal your hearts and home. Seek My face and see if I don't reward you. That came from the Lord, not me.

A few tears dropped from Cynthia's eyes. James reached out and wiped them away. "Thank you for the prayer," the woman said as they released hands, but Derek continued to hold onto Robyn's.

"If you don't attend church, I invite you to ours, Holy Ghost Temple. Our pastor preaches from the Bible and doesn't sugarcoat anything. Let God redeem you." She gave them the address.

"You two have been most encouraging." James nodded. "We'll visit your church soon," he said as the limo driver arrived in front of the restaurant.

"Trust me, there would have been no reconciliation if it wasn't for Jesus restoring our love for Him first."

"Yes," Robyn agreed. "As a matter of fact, we plan to get remarried on the anniversary of our divorce." She beamed, then Derek bid them good night and God's blessings.

Thirty-seven years was a long time to call it quits. If Robyn even hinted she was leaving, Derek planned to pack his bags and follow. This time, they would depend on Jesus to help them.

# CHAPTER SIXTEEN

The next morning, Derek hummed as he walked into his office. Robyn had awakened him, and they'd prayed together over the phone. It was more like rejoicing. Next, he let his family know the good news. Only his older brother seemed flabbergasted by the news.

"I can't believe you actually asked her again and Robyn said yes. I thought your cordiality was strictly for Tyler for Christmas." Marlon whistled. "I can't wrap my head around a Washington man clinching a forever love. Dad didn't find it…well he messed it up. I struck out…"

Derek stopped him before the pity party started. "I never wanted to be divorced. I let myself get in the way."

"Well, you're the family hero." His brother grunted. "Another man got in the way of my marriage."

"Then you evened the score," Derek reminded him. "That's called tit-for-tat, and Robyn and I played that game. We both got hurt in the end and our son got caught in the middle. Praise God for second chances. Do you think you'll ever get remarried?"

"Not while I'm still feeling the sting of my bruises my ex-wife left me. I mean what kind of mother leaves a good man and her children for the thrill?"

Derek knew the betrayal had cut him deep. *But Lord help my brother to see You in our lives this time,* he silently prayed. "Miracles do happen on Christmas. Jesus paid it all."

Marlon cut him off. "Enough Jesus talk. I'm really happy for you, bro. I really am, but Tammy and I are a done deal. When she gets out of prison for buying a gun and trying to kill me while putting the girls in harm's way, she can wreak havoc on that sorry boyfriend she cheated on me with."

With two little girls, Marlon wanted to have a full-time wife and mother for his daughters. Their grandmas could only do so much. "Jesus hasn't skipped over you. Take your concerns to Him and seek what gifts he has for you, and you won't have to wait for Christmas Day to open them."

"Yeah, right." After a few more minutes, they disconnected so Derek could make the call he had been itching to.

When Judge Wilson's clerk answered, he introduced himself, then shared his good news. "So I was hoping Judge Wilson will marry us."

"I'm sorry. She doesn't perform private weddings," Carla, Karen, Kay or whatever the lady's name advised him, crashing his morning.

"I don't think you understand. She granted my divorce, and I thought it would be a nice gesture for her to bind us together again," he pressed, wanting her to understand the significance of their request. People remarrying each other wasn't the norm—or was it?

The woman sighed. "I'm sorry. Judge Wilson's docket is full for the next month, and this is an unusual request."

Deflated, Derek was silent, not knowing what else to say while the clerk tapped on the computer keyboard. He had to talk to Robyn about a Plan B. "Okay, thanks."

"Hold on. Let me see… She's on the rotating schedule for the last March Wednesday wedding, but it won't be private. It's open to the public and on a first-come-first-serve basis."

After thanking her, he phoned Robyn and repeated the scenario. "I was hoping for something personal and to exchange vows on or before the anniversary of our divorce."

"Me too." She was silent. "I was thinking about that couple we met last night. Maybe our marriage is bigger than us. I couldn't believe we were encouraging the Websters versus them giving us nuggets of wisdom for long lasting marriages."

"I know. I said a prayer for them this morning."

"Maybe this public wedding isn't a bad idea," Robyn said with excitement in her voice. "The whole purpose of witnesses at a wedding is to share our happiness. I really want Judge Wilson to see what God has joined together will forever be together. Let's do it."

*Let's not,* Derek wanted to say. Hadn't he waited long enough for Robyn, but now the end of March? That added three more weeks of torture, but like she said, their second marriage was about God getting the glory. Together they were growing in God's wisdom. "Okay, sweetheart. I'll get the details."

Robyn was at peace remarrying Derek. Excited that his father would move into their home again, Tyler had stopped talking about wanting a puppy.

"Will God give me a baby brother or sister?" he asked one night before saying his prayers.

She wasn't about to ask her son how he knew about babies. "I hope so." It would be off her desire of two more children two years apart, but she was hopeful God would bless her womb again.

On March first, Robyn and Derek burned their divorce certificate and celebrated it with a loving kiss over a candlelight dinner. A week later, Elder Kinder began the first of three marriage counseling sessions.

"The word 'prodigal' can refer to anyone who comes to himself or herself and realizes grass is not always greener on the other side. Like the father in Luke 15 who lost his younger son to the cares of this world and rejoiced when the son came to his senses and returned home, the angels are rejoicing along with the Lord that you two have come to yourself. I plan to be in that courtroom to witness that grand occasion."

A few weeks later, James and Cynthia Webster visited Holy Ghost Temple. "Your pastor sounds like a wise man. We'll be back." James grinned.

"We would love to have you," Robyn said. "You are also invited to see us renew our vows at the courthouse."

Cynthia grabbed her husband's hand. "We wouldn't miss it."

On the last Wednesday of March, Robyn was surprised at the number of couples to be wed. It was done on a first come, first serve basis by way of numbers. It didn't matter as friends and family, plus their pastor, squeezed into the crowded courtroom.

It seemed fitting to have Tyler as their ring bearer, and he was beside himself with excitement.

Robyn watched as couples, many of them in regular clothes, were married in five minutes or less. A few kissed, some hugged, others simply walked away grinning. It seemed so impersonal, since she had dressed for the occasion in a pastel lilac dress, carried a small bouquet of lilies, and couldn't wait to kiss Derek as her husband.

"I've never been to a wedding before," Tyler whispered loudly from their perch on the back row.

She smiled at her son, who was dressed in a gray suit and lavender bow tie like his father. "I told you to marry Mommy, Daddy."

"And you were right, buddy," Derek said as he pulled Robyn closer with Tyler between them.

"Number twenty-four," the older, overweight bailiff finally announced.

Their group stood. She, Derek, and Tyler walked toward the judge as the bailiff encouraged her family to gather around for pictures and to act as witnesses.

After handing over the envelope that contained their unsigned license, Robyn exhaled. This was it.

The judge barely greeted them as she verified their names on the license. "Robyn Washington and Derek Washington."

"Yes," they said in unison.

"No relations?" She looked up and lifted an eyebrow. Robyn wondered if the judge would recognize them.

"Actually, we were married before and you granted our divorce," Derek explained.

She blinked, but her expression didn't change. "Well, I hope things will be better this second time around." Her smile seemed forced, which irked Robyn. Why wasn't the woman happy for them?

Derek must have sensed the same vibes too. "Put it this way, after we walk out of here today, we won't be needing your services," he stated, keeping his gaze on Robyn.

There were a few snickers and claps from the audience.

"That's my mom and dad," Tyler spoke up. "Jesus told me He was going to marry them, but you don't look like God."

The judge's expression softened with a slight surprised frown. "I'm not a god. I'm the Honorable Judge Deborah Wilson"

Their son's eyes widened. "But you work for God."

Judge Wilson seemed unsure how to respond, so she looked from Robyn and Derek for guidance.

Tyler frowned. "My teacher says Deborah was a smart lady judge in the Old Testament. She was wise…"

Praise God for the Christian school, but there was a time and place, so Robyn rested her hand on his shoulder to quiet him.

"No, let him finish," Judge Wilson said, seemingly amused. She squatted to Tyler's eye level and listened as he summarized the prophetess' role in Judges 4.

"She was a hero." Tyler jumped and dropped the pillow that had their rings attached. He eyed his parents. "Sorry." He picked it up, then stood at attention.

Standing also, the judge's countenance seemed different. Either Tyler impressed her with his Biblical understanding or she realized what a responsibility she had presiding over man-made laws.

"Dearly beloved, we are gathered here today to rejoin Robyn Washington to Derek Washington..." Judge Wilson began.

That wasn't the same generic spiel she had others recite, Robyn noted. Also, the coldness in her tone was gone. Her words weren't as harsh, and warmth engulfed Robyn as she looked into Derek's mesmerizing eyes.

"By the power vested in me by the state of Missouri and God," she said, then winked at Tyler, "I now pronounce you husband and wife. You may kiss your..."

Derek didn't wait, as he swiftly gathered Robyn in his arms and saluted her. The courtroom erupted into applause, whistles, and cheers. Two officers appeared to check on the ruckus at the same time Robyn threw her bouquet. It landed in Marlon's hands. Derek's brother hurriedly gave it to his oldest daughter, then snatched it back, realizing the significance.

Robyn and Derek laughed. It appeared God was about to continue to do restoration in the family.

# EPILOGUE

Nine months later, two days after Tyler's seventh and Christ's birthday, Robyn delivered a baby girl. Tyler insisted they name her Deborah.

"I guess everything worked out the way it was supposed too, huh?" she asked her husband as she cuddled their infant in her arms.

"In what way, babe?" He hadn't left her side during her many hours of labor.

"We celebrate Christ's birth on Christmas, but...the rebirth of our marriage began last Christmas, and this year, Christ gave us new life. Plus, since I stayed with the firm, my severance pay just ran out."

Derek chuckled. "I was going to take care of you anyway. You know my brother's jealous of us. He's looking for Jesus to bring him a gift with nice legs."

Robyn smiled. With God's sense of humor, Jesus just might do that.

# AUTHOR'S NOTE

If Robyn, Derek, and Tyler have warmed your heart this holiday season, please take a moment and write a review on Amazon and Goodreads, and share it with other book lovers. Also, consider gifting a copy as a present. May God bless you for blessing me.

Don't forget to stop by www.patsimmons.net. Sign up for my newsletter and get a free download.

Coming this Valentine's Day, *Love for Delivery*.

Want more Christmas stories? Check out my other titles.

# BOOK CLUB DISCUSSION

1. What was the turning point for Robyn and Derek to reconsider marriage?
2. If you are divorced or have friends who are divorcees, discuss whether reconciliation was considered?
3. Talk about your favorite scene in the story?
4. Robyn thought she got married too young. In what ways do you think she was right, or wrong?
5. Discuss whether Derek's father, Tyrone, influenced Derek's mindset when it came to marriage.
6. In your opinion, can a young couple encourage older married folks like James and Cynthia?
7. How did Tyler bring his parents together, or did he?

# About the Author

Pat Simmons is the multi-published author of more than thirty Christian titles and is a three-time recipient of the Emma Rodgers Award for Best Inspirational Romance. She has been a featured speaker and workshop presenter at various venues across the country.

As a self-proclaimed genealogy sleuth, Pat is passionate about researching her ancestors and then casting them in starring roles in her novels. She describes the evidence of the gift of the Holy Ghost as an amazing, unforgettable, life-altering experience. God is the Author who advances the stories she writes.

Pat currently oversees the media publicity for the annual RT Booklovers Conventions. She has a B.S. in mass communications from Emerson College in Boston, Massachusetts.

Pat converted her sofa-strapped, sports-fanatic husband into an amateur travel agent, untrained bodyguard, GPS-guided chauffeur, and administrative assistant who is constantly on probation. They have a son and a daughter.

# OTHER CHRISTIAN TITLES

## The Guilty series

Book I: *Guilty of Love*

Book II: *Not Guilty of Love*

Book III: *Still Guilty*

Book IV: *The Acquittal*

## The Jamieson Legacy

Book I: *Guilty by Association*

Book II: *The Guilt Trip*

Book III: *Free from Guilt*

Book IV: *The Confession*

## The Carmen Sisters

Book I: *No Easy Catch*

Book II: *In Defense of Love*

Book III: *Driven to Be Loved*

Book IV: *Redeeming Heart*

**Love at the Crossroads**

Book I: *Stopping Traffic*

Book II: *A Baby for Christmas*

Book III: *The Keepsake*

Book IV: *What God Has for Me*

Book V: *Every Woman Needs a Praying Man*

**Making Love Work Anthology**

Book I: *Love at Work*

Book II: *Words of Love*

Book III: *A Mother's Love*

*Pat Simmons*

**Restore My Soul series**

*Crowning Glory*

*Jet: The Back Story*

*Love Led by the Spirit*

**Single Titles**

*Talk to Me*

*Her Dress* (novella)

**Holiday Titles**

Andersen Brothers series

Book I: *Love for the Holidays* (Three Christian novellas): *A Christian Christmas, A Christian Easter,* and *A Christian Father's Day*

# COUPLE BY CHRISTMAS

Book II: *A Woman After David's Heart* (Valentine's Day)

Book III: *A Noelle for Nathan*

*Christmas Greetings*

*Couple By Christmas*

# Restore My Soul series

***Crowning Glory***, Book 1. Cinderella had a prince; Karyn Wallace has a King. While Karyn served four years in prison for an unthinkable crime, she embraced salvation through Crowns for Christ outreach ministry. After her release, Karyn stays strong and confident, despite the stigma society places on ex-offenders. Since Christ strengthens the underdog, Karyn refuses to sway away from the scripture, "He who the Son has set free is free indeed." Levi Tolliver, for the most part, is a practicing Christian. One contradiction is he doesn't believe in turning the other cheek. He's steadfast there is a price to pay for every sin committed, especially after the untimely death of his wife during a robbery. Then Karyn enters Levi's life. He is enthralled not only with her beauty, but her sweet spirit until he learns about her incarceration. If Levi can accept that Christ paid Karyn's debt in full, then a treasure awaits him. This is a powerful tale and reminds readers of the permanency of redemption.

***Jet: The Back Story to Love Led By the Spirit***, Book 2. To say Jesetta "Jet" Hutchens has issues is an understatement. In Crowning Glory, Book 1 of the Restoring My Soul series, she releases a firestorm of anger with an unforgiving heart. But every hurting soul has a history. In Jet: The Back Story to Love Led by the Spirit, Jet doesn't know how to cope with the loss of her younger sister, Diane.

But God sets her on the road to a spiritual recovery. To make sure she doesn't get lost, Jesus sends the handsome and single Minister Rossi Tolliver to be her guide.

Psalm 147:3 says Jesus can heal the brokenhearted and bind up their wounds. That sets the stage for Love Led by the Spirit.

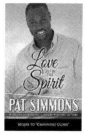

***Love Led By the Spirit,*** Book 3. Minister Rossi Tolliver is ready to settle down. Besides the outwardly attraction, he desires a woman who is sweet, humble, and loves church folks. Sounds simple enough on paper, but when he gets off his knees, praying for that special someone to come into his life, God opens his eyes to the woman who has been there all along. There is only a slight problem. Love is the farthest thing from Jesetta "Jet" Hutchens' mind. But Rossi, the man and the minister, is hard to resist. Is Jet ready to allow the Holy Spirit to lead her to love?

# LOVE AT THE CROSSROADS SERIES

***Stopping Traffic,*** Book 1. Candace Clark has a phobia about crossing the street, and for good reason. As fate would have it, her daughter's principal assigns her to crossing guard duties as part of the school's Parent Participation program. With no choice in the matter, Candace begrudgingly accepts her stop sign and safety vest, then reports to her designated crosswalk. Once Candace is determined to overcome her fears, God opens the door for a blessing, and Royce Kavanaugh enters into her life, a firefighter built to rescue any damsel in distress. When a spark of attraction ignites, Candace and Royce soon discover there's more than one way to stop traffic

***A Baby For Christmas***, Book 2. Yes, diamonds are a girl's best friend, but in Solae Wyatt-Palmer's case, she desires something more valuable. Captain Hershel Kavanaugh is a divorcee and the father of two adorable little boys. Solae has never been married and longs to be a mother. Although Hershel showers her with expensive gifts, his hesitation about proposing causes Solae to walk and never look back. As the holidays approach, Hershel must convince Solae that she has everything he could ever want for Christmas

**The Keepsake**, Book 3. Until death us do part...or until Desiree walks away. Desiree "Desi" Bishop is devastated when she finds evidence of her husband's affair. God knew she didn't get married only to one day have to stand before a judge and file for a divorce. But Desi wants out no matter how much her heart says to forgive Michael. That isn't easier said than done. She sees God's one acceptable reason for a divorce as the only opt-out clause in her marriage. Michael Bishop is a repenting man who loves his wife of three years. If only...he had paid attention to the red flags God sent to keep him from falling into the devil's snares. But Michael didn't and he had fallen. Although God had forgiven him instantly when he repented, Desi's forgiveness is moving as a snail's pace. In the end, after all the tears have been shed and forgiveness granted and received, the couple learns that some marriages are worth keeping

**What God Has For Me**, Book 4. Halcyon Holland is leaving her live-in boyfriend, taking their daughter and the baby in her belly with her. She's tired of waiting for the ring, so she buys herself one. When her ex doesn't reconcile their relationship, Halcyon begins to second-guess whether or not she compromised her chance for a happily ever after. After all, what man in his right mind would want to deal with the community stigma of 'baby mama drama?' But Zachary Bishop has had his eye on Halcyon since the first time he saw her. Without a ring on her finger, Zachary prays that she will come to her senses and not only leave Scott, but come back to God. What one man doesn't cherish, Zach is ready to treasure. Not deterred by Halcyon's broken spirit,

Zachary is on a mission to offer her a second chance at love that she can't refuse. And as far as her adorable children are concerned, Zachary's love is unconditional for a ready-made family. Halcyon will soon learn that her past circumstances won't hinder the Lord's blessings, because what God has for her, is for her...and him...and the children.

***Every Woman Needs A Praying Man***, Book 5. First impressions can make or break a business deal and they definitely could be a relationship buster, but an ill-timed panic attack draws two strangers together. Unlike firefighters who run into danger, instincts tell businessman Tyson Graham to head the other way as fast as he can when he meets a certain damsel in distress. Days later, the same woman struts through his door for a job interview. Monica Wyatt might possess the outwardly beauty and the brains on paper, but Tyson doesn't trust her to work for his firm, or maybe he doesn't trust his heart around her.

***A Christian Christmas***. Christian's Christmas will never be the same for Joy Knight if Christian Andersen has his way. Not to be confused with a secret Santa, Christian and his family are busier than Santa's elves making sure the Lord's blessings are distributed to those less fortunate by Christmas day. Joy is playing the hand that life dealt her, rearing four children in a home that is on the brink of foreclosure. She's not looking for a handout, but when Christian rescues her in the checkout line; her niece thinks Christian is an angel. Joy thinks he's just another man who will eventually leave, disappointing her and the children. Although Christian is a servant of the Lord, he is a flesh and blood man and all he wants for Christmas is Joy Knight. Can time spent with Christian turn Joy's attention from her financial woes to the real meaning of Christmas—and true love?

***A Christian Easter***., How to celebrate Easter becomes a balancing act for Christian and Joy Andersen and their four children. Chocolate bunnies, colorful stuffed baskets and flashy fashion shows are their competition. Despite the enticements, Christian refuses to succumb without a fight. And it becomes a tug of war when his recently adopted ten year-old daughter, Bethani, wants to participate in her friend's Easter tradition. Christian hopes he has instilled Proverbs 22:6, into the children's heart in the short time of being their dad.

***A Christian Father's Day***. Three fathers, one Father's Day and four children. Will the real dad, please stand up. It's never too late to be a father—or is it? Christian Andersen was looking forward to spending his first Father's day with his adopted children---all four of them. But Father's day becomes more complicated than Christian or Joy ever imagined. Christian finds himself faced with living up to his name when things don't go his way to enjoy an idyllic once a year celebration. But he depends on God to guide him through the journey. (All three of Christian's individual stories are in the Love for the Holidays anthology (Book 1 of the Andersen Brothers series)

***A Woman After David's Heart***, Book 2, David Andersen doesn't have a problem indulging in Valentine's Day, per se, but not on a first date. Considering it was the love fest of the year, he didn't want a woman to get any ideas that a wedding ring was forthcoming before he got a chance to know her. So he has no choice but to wait until the whole Valentine's Day hoopla was over, then he would make his move on a sister in his church he can't take his eyes off of. For the past two years and counting, Valerie Hart hasn't been the recipient of a romantic Valentine's Day dinner invitation. To fill the void, Valerie keeps herself busy with God's business, hoping the Lord will send her perfect mate soon. Unfortunately, with no prospects in sight, it looks like that won't happen again this year. A Woman After David's Heart is a Valentine romance novella that can be enjoyed with or without a box of chocolates.

**A Noelle For Nathan**, Book 3, is a story of kindness, selflessness, and falling in love during the Christmas season. Andersen Investors & Consultants, LLC, CFO Nathan Andersen (A Christian Christmas) isn't looking for attention when he buys a homeless man a meal, but grade school teacher Noelle Foster is watching his every move with admiration. His generosity makes him a man after her own heart. While donors give more to children and families in need around the holiday season, Noelle Foster believes in giving year-round after seeing many of her students struggle with hunger and finding a warm bed at night. At a second-chance meeting, sparks fly when Noelle and Nathan share a kindred spirit with their passion to help those less fortunate. Whether they're doing charity work or attending Christmas parties, the couple becomes inseparable. Although Noelle and Nathan exchange gifts, the biggest present is the one from Christ.

# MAKING LOVE WORK SERIES

*A Mother's Love.* To Jillian Carter, it's bad when her own daughter beats her to the altar. She became a teenage mother when she confused love for lust one summer. Despite the sins of her past, Jesus forgave her and blessed her to be the best Christian example for Shana. Jillian is not looking forward to becoming an empty-nester at thirty-nine. The old adage, she's not losing a daughter, but gaining a son-in-law is not comforting as she braces for a lonely life ahead. What she doesn't expect is for two men to vie for her affections: Shana's biological father who breezes back into their lives as a redeemed man and practicing Christian. Not only is Alex still goof looking, but he's willing to right the wrong he's done in the past. Not if Dr. Dexter Harris has anything to say about it. The widower father of the groom has set his sights on Jillian and he's willing to pull out all the stops to woo her. Now the choice is hers. Who will be the next mother's love?

*Love At Work.* How do two people go undercover to hide an office romance in a busy television newsroom? In plain sight, of course. Desiree King is an assignment editor at KDPX-TV in St. Louis, MO. She dispatches a team to wherever breaking news happens. Her focus is to stay ahead of the competition. Overall, she's easy-going, respectable, and compassionate. But when it comes to dating a fellow coworker, she refuses to cross that professional line. Award-winning investigative reporter Bryan Mitchell makes life challenging for Desiree with his thoughtful gestures, sweet notes, and support. He tries to convince Desiree that as Christians, they could show coworkers how to blend their personal and private lives without compromising their morals.

***Words Of Love***. Call it old fashion, but Simone French was smitten with a love letter. Not a text, email, or Facebook post, but a love letter sent through snail mail. The prose wasn't the corny roses-are-red-and-violets-are-blue stuff. The first letter contained short accolades for a job well done. Soon after, the missives were filled with passionate words from a man who confessed the hidden secrets of his soul. He revealed his unspoken weaknesses, listed his uncompromising desires, and unapologetically noted his subtle strengths. Yes, Rice Taylor was ready to surrender to love. Whew. Closing her eyes, Simone inhaled the faint lingering smell of roses on the beige plain stationery. She had a testimony. If anyone would listen, she would proclaim that love was truly blind.

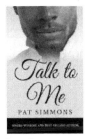

***Talk To Me***. Despite being deaf as a result of a fireworks explosion, CEO of a St. Louis non-profit company, Noel Richardson, expertly navigates the hearing world. What some view as a disability, Noel views as a challenge—his lack of hearing has never held him back. It also helps that he has great looks, numerous university degrees, and full bank accounts. But those assets don't define him as a man who longs for the right woman in his life. Deciding to visit a church service, Noel is blind-sided by the most beautiful and graceful Deaf interpreter he's ever seen. Mackenzie Norton challenges him on every level through words and signing, but as their love grows, their faith is tested. When their church holds a yearly revival, they witness the healing power of God in others. Mackenzie has faith to believe that Noel can also get in on the blessing. Since faith comes by hearing, whose voice does Noel hear in his heart, Mackenzie or God's?

TESTIMONY: ***If I Should Die Before I Wake.*** It is of the LORD's mercies that we are not consumed, because His compassions fail not. They are new every morning, great is Thy faithfulness. Lamentations 3:22-23, God's mercies are sure; His promises are fulfilled; but a dawn of a new morning is God' grace. If you need a testimony about God's grace, then If I Should Die Before I Wake will encourage your soul. Nothing happens in our lives by chance. If you need a miracle, God's got that too. Trust Him. Has it been a while since you've had a testimony? Increase your prayer life, build your faith and walk in victory because without a test, there is no testimony. (ebook only)

***Her Dress***. Sometimes a woman just wants to splurge on something new, especially when she's about to attend an event with movers and shakers. Find out what happens when Pepper Trudeau is all dressed up and goes to the ball, but another woman is modeling the same attire. At first, Pepper is embarrassed, then the night gets interesting when she meets Drake Logan. Her Dress is a romantic novella about the all too common occurrence—two women shopping at the same place. Maybe having the same taste isn't all bad. Sometimes a good dress is all you need to meet the man of your dreams. (ebook only)

Saige Carter loves everything about Christmas: the shopping, the food, the lights, and of course, Christmas wouldn't be complete without family and friends to share in the traditions they've created together. Plus, Saige is extra excited about her line of Christmas greeting cards hitting store shelves, but when she gets devastating news around the holidays, she wonders if she'll ever look at Christmas the same again. Daniel Washington is no Scrooge, but he'd rather skip the holidays altogether than spend them with his estranged family. After one too many arguments around the dinner table one year, Daniel had enough and walked away from the drama. As one year has turned into many, no one seems willing to take the first step toward reconciliation. When Daniel reads one of Saige's greeting cards, he's unsure if the words inside are enough to erase the pain and bring about forgiveness. Once God reveals to them

His purpose for their lives, they will have a reason to rejoice.

Holidays haven't been the same for Derek Washington since his divorce. He and his ex-wife, Robyn, go out the way to avoid each other. This Christmas may be different when he decides to gives his son, Tyler, the family he once had before the split. Derek's going to need the Lord's intervention to soften his ex-wife's heart to agree. God's help doesn't come in the way he expected, but it's all good, because everything falls in place for them to be a couple by Christmas.

# THE GUILTY SERIES KICK OFF

 ***Guilty of Love***. When do you know the most important decision of your life is the right one? Reaping the seeds from what she's sown; Cheney Reynolds moves into a historic neighborhood in Ferguson, Missouri, and becomes a reclusive. Her first neighbor, the incomparable Mrs. Beatrice Tilley Beacon aka Grandma BB, is an opinionated childless widow. Grandma BB is a self-proclaimed expert on topics Cheney isn't seeking advice—everything from landscaping to hip-hop dancing to romance. Then there is Parke Kokumuo Jamison VI, a direct descendant of a royal African tribe. He learned his family ancestry, African history, and lineage preservation before he could count. Unwittingly, they are drawn to each other, but it takes Christ to weave their lives into a spiritual bliss while He exonerates their past indiscretions.

 ***Not Guilty***. One man, one woman, one God and one big problem. Malcolm Jamieson wasn't the man who got away, but the man God instructed Hallison Dinkins to set free. Instead of their explosive love affair leading them to the wedding altar, God diverted Hallison to the prayer altar during her first visit back to church in years. Malcolm was convinced that his woman had loss her mind to break off their engagement. Didn't Hallison know that Malcolm, a tenth generation descendant of a royal African tribe, couldn't be replaced? Once Malcolm concedes that their relationship can't be savaged, he issues Hallison his own edict, "If we're meant to be with each other, we'll find our

way back. If not, that means that there's a love stronger than what we had." His words begin to haunt Hallison until she begins to regret their break up, and that's where their story begins. Someone has to retreat, and God never loses a battle.

***Still Guilty***. Cheney Reynolds Jamieson made a choice years ago that is now shaping her future and the future of the men she loves. A botched abortion left her unable to carry a baby to term, and her husband, Parke K. Jamison VI, is expected to produce heirs. With a wife who cannot give him a child, Parke vows to find and get custody of his illegitimate son by any means necessary. Meanwhile, Cheney's twin brother, Rainey, struggles with his anger over his ex-girlfriend's actions that haunt him, and their father, Dr. Roland Reynolds, fights to keep an old secret in the past.

***The Acquittal***. Two worlds apart, but their hearts dance to the same African drum beat. On a professional level, Dr. Rainey Reynolds is a competent, highly sought-after orthodontist. Inwardly, he needs to be set free from the chaos of revelations that make him question if happiness is obtainable. To get away from the drama, Rainey is willing to leave the country under the guise of a mission trip with Dentist Without Borders. Will changing his surroundings really change him? If one woman can heal his wounds, then he will believe that there is really peace after the storm. Ghanaian beauty Josephine Abena Yaa Amoah returns to Africa after completing her studies as an exchange student in St. Louis, Missouri. Although her heart bleeds for his peace, she knows she must step back and pray for Rainey's surrender to Christ in order for God to acquit him of his self-inflicted mental torture. In the Motherland of Ghana, Africa, Rainey not only visits the places of his ancestors, will he embrace the liberty that Christ's Blood really does set every man free.

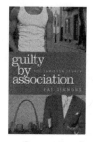

***Guilty By Association***. How important is a name? To the St. Louis Jamiesons who are tenth generation descendants of a royal African tribe—everything. To the Boston Jamiesons whose father never married their mother—there is no loyalty or legacy. Kidd Jamieson suffers from the "angry" male syndrome because his father was an absent in the home, but insisted his two sons carry his last name. It takes an old woman who mingles genealogy truths and Bible verses together for Kidd to realize his worth as a strong black man. He learns it's not his association with the name that identifies him, but the man he becomes that defines him.

***The Guilt Trip***. Aaron "Ace" Jamieson is living a carefree life. He's good-looking, respectable when he's in the mood, but his weakness is women. If a woman tries to ambush him with a pregnancy, he takes off in the other direction. It's a lesson learned from his absentee father that responsibility is optional. Talise Rogers has a bright future ahead of her. She's pretty and has no problem catching a man's eye, which is exactly what she does with Ace. Trapping Ace Jamieson is the furthest thing from Taleigh's mind when she learns she pregnant and Ace rejects her. "I want nothing from you Ace, not even your name." And Talise meant it.

***Free From Guilt***. It's salvation round-up time and Cameron Jamieson's name is on God's hit list. Although his brothers and cousins embraced God—thanks to the women in their lives—the two-degreed MIT graduate isn't going to let any woman take him down that path without a fight. He's satisfied with his career, social calendar, and good genes. But God uses a beautiful messenger, Gabrielle Dupree, to show him that he's in a spiritual deficit. Cameron learns the hard way that man's wisdom is like foolishness to God. For every philosophical argument he throws her way, Gabrielle exposes him to scriptures that makes him question his worldly knowledge.

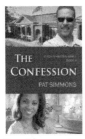

***The Confession***. Sandra Nicholson had made good and bad choices throughout the years, but the best one was to give her life to Christ when her sons were small and to rear them up in the best Christian way she knew how. That was thirty something years ago and Sandra has evolved from a young single mother of two rambunctious boys, Kidd and Ace Jamieson, to a godly woman seasoned with wisdom. Despite the challenges and trials of rearing two strong-willed personalities, Sandra maintained her sanity through the grace of God, which kept gray strands at bay. Now, Sandra Nicholson is on the threshold of happiness, but Kidd believes no man is good enough for his mother, especially if her love interest could be a man just like his absentee father.

***No Easy Catch***. Shae Carmen hasn't lost her faith in God, only the men she's come across. Shae's recent heartbreak was discovering that her boyfriend was not only married, but on the verge of reconciling with his estranged wife. Humiliated, Shae begins to second guess herself as why she didn't see the signs that he was nothing more than a devil's decoy masquerading as a devout Christian man. St. Louis Outfielder Rahn Maxwell finds himself a victim of an attempted carjacking. The Lord guides him out of harms' way by opening the gunmen's eyes to Rahn's identity. The crook instead becomes infatuated fan and asks for Rahn's autograph, and as a good will gesture, directs Rahn out of the ambush! When the news media gets wind of what happened with the baseball player, Shae's television station lands an exclusive interview. Shae and Rahn's chance meeting sets in motion a relationship where Rahn not only surrenders to Christ, but pursues Shae with a purpose to prove that good men are still out there. After letting her guard down, Shae is faced with another scandal that rocks her world. This time the stakes are higher. Not only is her heart on the line, so is her professional credibility. She and Rahn are at odds as how to handle it and friction erupts between them. Will she strike out at love again? The Lord shows Rahn that nothing happens by chance, and everything is done for Him to get the glory.

***In Defense of Love***. Lately, nothing in Garrett Nash's life has made sense. When two people close to the U.S. Marshal wrong him deeply, Garrett expects God to remove them from his life. Instead, the Lord relocates Garrett to another city to start over, as if he were the offender instead of the victim. Criminal attorney Shari Carmen is comfortable in her own skin—most of the time. Being a "dark and lovely" African-American sister has its challenges, especially when it comes to relationships. Although she's a fireball in the courtroom, she knows how to fade into the background and keep the proverbial spotlight off her personal life. But literal spotlights are a different matter altogether. While playing tenor saxophone at an anniversary party, she grabs the attention of Garrett Nash. And as God draws them closer together, He makes another request of Garrett, one to which it will prove far more difficult to say "Yes, Lord."

***Redeeming Heart***. Landon Thomas (In Defense of Love) brings a new definition to the word "prodigal," as in prodigal son, brother or anything else imaginable. It's a good thing that God's love covers a multitude of sins, but He isn't letting Landon off easy. His journey from riches to rags proves to be humbling and a lesson well learned. Real Estate Agent Octavia Winston is a woman on a mission, whether it's God's or hers professionally. One thing is for certain, she's not about to compromise when it comes to a Christian mate, so why did God send a homeless man to steal her heart? Minister Rossi Tolliver (Crowning Glory) knows how to minister to God's lost sheep and through God's redemption, the game changes for Landon and Octavia

**Driven to Be Loved.** On the surface, Brecee Carmen has nothing in common with Adrian Cole. She is a pediatrician certified in trauma care; he is a transportation problem solver for a luxury car dealership (a.k.a., a car salesman). Despite their slow but steady attraction to each other, neither one of them are sure that they're compatible. To complicate matters, Brecee is the sole unattached Carmen when it seems as though everyone else around her—family and friends—are finding love, except her.

Through a series of discoveries, Adrian and Brecee learn that things don't happen by coincidence. Generational forces are at work, keeping promises, protecting family members, and perhaps even drawing Adrian back to the church. For Brecee and Adrian, God has been hard at work, playing matchmaker all along the way for their paths cross at the right time and the right place.

Check out my fellow Christian fiction authors writing about faith, family and love. You won't be disappointed.

www.blackchristianreads.com

Made in the USA
Middletown, DE
03 December 2016